TIPSY

(a *Take It Off* novel)

Julie Preston is an artist. But her canvas isn't paper or clay. It's hair. She spends her days coloring, blow drying and styling her clients hair at the Razor's Edge salon. Julie is also annoyed. She went out on a date and had a great time, gave the guy her number and the jerk never called.

So when he waltzes into the salon and sits down in her chair she briefly considers strangling him with the pink cape she fastens around his neck.

Too bad she can't.

Blue Markson, the guy who never called, is a police officer so causing him bodily harm would be a first class ticket into the slammer. Just looking at him again makes Julie forget why she was mad in the first place, but she's already learned that Blue is nothing but heartache. So when he starts coming around, acting like he hadn't made her stare at the phone for days, she tries to brush him off.

Only…

Her life is about to blow up in her face, she's about to get caught up in a sticky web of crime and the one guy who can help her is the one guy she vowed never to trust again.

TIPSY

Take It Off Series

CAMBRIA HEBERT

Published by: Cambria Hebert

http://www.cambriahebert.com

Interior design and typesetting by Sharon Kay
Cover design by MAE I DESIGN
Edited by Cassie McCown
Copyright 2013 by Cambria Hebert

ISBN: 978-1-938857-36-2

Other books by Cambria Hebert

Heven and Hell Series

Before

Masquerade

Between

Charade

Bewitched

Tirade

Beneath

Renegade

Heven & Hell Anthology

Death Escorts

Recalled

Charmed

Take It Off

Torch

Tease

Tempt

Text

DEDICATION

This book is dedicated to those I consider part of my team. These are the people who make my books readable, pretty, and better than I could ever make them alone. They make time out of their busy lives to edit, format, and design for me. This business can be a tough one, and I consider myself beyond fortunate that I have these reliable core people behind me to make sure my books are the best they can be.

Regina Wamba – Photography and Cover Design.
Cassie McCown – Editing
Sharon Kay – Formatting

I'd also like to dedicate this to my two consistent beta readers who always make time to catch any last minute errors and read through my drafts—sometimes at quick speeds.

Melissa Stickney
Stephanie Nicole Garza

TIPSY

PROLOGUE

Julie

How they met...

Morning from hell. I was not a morning person. I never was and I never would be. Getting up in the morning is pretty much the worst part of my day. Trying to drag myself out of a way comfortable bed where I'm surrounded by fluffy pillows and soft bedding is pretty much the epitome of torture.

Add an alarm that never shuts up, cold tile in the bathroom that feels like tiny needles being jammed into my skin, and you have the makings for a very bitchy Julie.

Thank goodness I lived alone. There was no way in hell any man could go up against the morning sunshine I projected.

To make matters worse, I was running late. I hated being late. If I was late to work, it would throw off every appointment I had that day, and I would spend every single hour trying to play catch-up.

I rushed around trying to get ready, pulling on a cotton dress because it was a hell of a lot harder to try and match clothes together when I was stumbling around like a living zombie. (Wait. Zombies didn't live. They were dead.) Then I cinched a red patent leather belt around my waist on my way down the stairs. I would have to do my eye makeup at work and I would also have to touch up my hair.

Glancing at the clock, I sighed and gave a longing glance at my kitchen, where the coffee was kept.

I didn't have time for caffeine. I felt sorry for everyone who had to deal with me.

I grabbed my purse and rushed out the door and climbed into my little silver car. The air was already thick and I knew soon the summer heat was going to bore down on this town like a hungry woman at Waffle House.

I turned out of my neighborhood and tore down the street, letting out an unladylike curse word when I got caught by a red light.

When it turned green, I sped around the corner and glanced at the clock. Five minutes.

Flashing blue lights had me glancing in the rearview mirror. More unladylike curses exploded from my mouth as I pulled to the side of the road and prayed the cop would speed by.

Of course he didn't.

He pulled to a stop behind me.

I so did not have time for this.

Why is it that police officers always picked on the innocent people who rarely ever speed, yet they never pull over the people who are complete assholes on the road all the time?

Maybe I would ask him.

He knocked on the window and I sighed. I wasn't even going try to talk my way out of this one. It would be safer if I kept my mouth shut. It certainly would be cheaper.

I pressed the button and my window rolled down.

"License and registration, please," said a voice from above.

I let out another huffing sigh and leaned over, digging around in my bag and glove compartment for the items, and thrust them out the window while staring straight ahead. I could practically feel all the other drivers laughing at me as they drove past.

It really didn't improve my caffeine-deprived mood.

A few minutes later, the police officer leaned down in the window. "Did you know you were violating the speed laws, ma'am?"

Forget being quiet. I couldn't do it. I opened my lips to give him a less-than-polite answer and turned my head.

Every single word fled my brain. I mean my vocabulary literally ran away. I couldn't even blame them. There was no word that could compete with such a face.

His eyes were such a deep blue that they held me captive in a single glance. He had a masculine and angular face, with a straight nose, full lips, and a cleft in the center of his chin. He was clean shaven and smelled so good that I actually leaned closer.

Who in the hell actually leaned closer to an officer who wanted to give her a speeding ticket?

He was lean but not too thin, tall, and did his uniform justice. I was a little embarrassed to admit the gun strapped to his hip turned me on.

And then I saw the handcuffs.

I didn't know I was a dirty ho until that moment. I imagined all kinds of inappropriate things involving those handcuffs.

He took off his hat and ran his hand through his hair. "Ma'am?"

I glanced at him, once again struck by his eyes. I felt the need to lean even closer, but I stopped myself.

"What?" I said, the word coming out a little harsher than I intended.

I swear he stifled a smile. "You were speeding..." he said, trailing away.

I couldn't stop staring at the little dent in his chin. My tongue would fit in it perfectly. I cleared my throat. "I'm late for work."

The statement brought me back to reality. "Shit!" I yelled, hitting the steering wheel. "I'm late for work."

I winced and turned back to him. "Are you going to arrest me now?"

He laughed. He actually threw his head back and laughed.

God, he was sexy.

"Where do you work?"

"Right up the street at Razor's Edge."

"You make a habit out of speeding through an intersection?"

I made a frustrated sound. "Only on days I don't get my coffee, have to get out of bed at ungodly hours and..." Oh, crap, there I went again. I looked at him meekly. "No?"

"No coffee, huh?"

"No," I grumped.

He sighed and straightened. He pulled a pad out of his pocket and then proceeded to write on it. I wondered how much this was going to cost me.

A minute later, he handed back my ID and registration. I put them away and turned back to collect my sentence.

He was putting the notepad back in his pocket.

"Isn't that for me?"

He leaned back down in the window, bracing his forearms on the side of the car. "Nope. It's for me."

I felt my forehead crease. "I know I'm not properly caffeinated, but don't people who speed usually get tickets?"

"Usually," he agreed.

I lifted my eyebrows. I was back to being mute. He was incredibly close.

"I'm going to let you off with a warning this time."

I made a sound that might have come across as an agreement.

He grinned. "On one condition."

I scowled. "I read an article about this once. Officers of the law letting people go in exchange for… *favors*."

He chuckled. "Is that so?"

I crossed my arms over my chest. "I'm not that kind of a girl, Officer Shady."

He lifted an eyebrow and I felt my cheeks heat. *That's good, Julie. Insult a cop.*

"Are you the kind of girl who would go on a date with a shady police officer?"

My hands broke out in a clammy sweat. Did he just ask me out? "That depends," I said saucily.

What the hell is wrong with me this morning?

The rate my day was going, I was going to shave off someone's eyebrow and turn their hair green.

"On?"

"How many times this admitted shady cop has pulled women over to ask them out on dates."

He flashed a smile and my heart stuttered. "Never."

I wasn't sure I believed that, but I wanted to. "If I agree, will you let me go to work?"

"Yep."

"Okay, then."

He smiled again and straightened, putting on his hat. "Watch your speed," he said, tapping the side of my door with his fingers.

"Don't you want my number?"

He leaned down once more. "Already got it. What do you think I was writing down?"

"I'm pretty sure that's abuse of your job."

He chuckled. "You gonna call my boss and rat me out?"

Hell no, I wasn't. "Maybe."

"I don't think so," he said softly.

"What makes you so sure?"

"Because, Julie," he drawled, and I swear my name on his lips made me lightheaded. "You want to go out with me."

I did. But I wasn't going to tell him that. He was already suffering from an oversized ego. "You going tell me your name?"

"Blue," he said, stepping back from my car.

I'd never heard that name before. But considering the pull of his eyes, I understood it.

"Well, Blue, I guess I'll see ya when I see ya."

"Oh, you'll see me. Tonight. I'll pick you up at six."

Tonight? He worked fast. Maybe he should get a speeding ticket.

I waited until he was in his cruiser before I pulled out onto the road. He pulled out behind me and followed my car the entire way to the salon. When I pulled in the lot, he kept going and I blew out a nervous breath.

I needed to revise my earlier statement. It was no longer the morning from hell.

For once, I was actually glad I got my ass of bed.

1

Julie

Several months later…

The guy that never called? I was staring at him. How unfortunate for him I was holding scissors.

I thought for sure the minute he laid eyes on me and my potential weapon, he would turn tail and run. He wasn't very smart, which he proved when he never called (clearly, his loss) and then again when instead of walking away, he came closer.

He smiled as if flashing his perfectly straight, white teeth would make me swoon.

My days of swooning over him were over.

Candy, the flighty receptionist, wasn't immune to his oozing good looks, casual charm, and smooth-talking self. She all but drooled when she waved her hand in my direction.

I narrowed my eyes when he lazily strolled over to me, his hips rotating as he kicked out his jean-clad thighs and his worn T-shirt brushed against the low-riding waistband. He didn't say anything as he lowered himself in the black swivel chair in front of me.

"What do you want?" I snapped when he only stared at me with his deep blue eyes through the mirror.

He looked pointedly at the scissors in my hand. "A haircut," he said like it was obvious, flashing that grin again. "That is what you do, isn't it?"

I thought about stabbing him. Like seriously stabbing him.

I snapped the gum I wasn't supposed to be chewing and smiled. I had to behave; management was watching. I couldn't afford to be seen disrespecting a law enforcement officer.

"Where's your uniform?" I asked, arching a perfectly waxed brow at him.

He gave me a sly smile. "Left it at home. Didn't want to give any of the ladies here heart failure today."

Then he winked.

Dammit. It was sexy.

I rolled my eyes, refusing to acknowledge the fact that he was indeed a hot bad boy who was actually good. I turned my back and reached toward the hook and pulled off a fuscia cape to drape around his neck.

"Pink?" he said, lifting a brow.

"I spilled something all over my black one. Oops! If you want to go somewhere else, I totally understand."

He smirked. "Nope. I'm already here."

I fastened the Velcro a little tighter around his neck than need be. He lifted a brow again, and I shrugged. "Wouldn't want you to get all hairy." I batted my lashes.

He snorted.

I expelled a quiet breath and silently told myself to get it together. He was a client. He needed a haircut. It would be over in ten minutes and then he'd leave.

I didn't want to touch him.

I had to.

Instead of getting right to work, I forced my eyes up and looked at his reflection in the large mirror hanging over my workstation. His brown hair had grown longer since our one and only date. It was shaggy and hung over his ears and forehead. The back brushed against the cape.

The last I saw him, it was shorter. Cut around his ears, short on the sides, and a little length on the top, which he mostly wore messy (no doubt because he didn't bother combing it).

I rested my palms on the back of the chair. "So what's up with your hair?"

"I haven't had the chance to get it cut in a while," he said, keeping those deep azure eyes trained on me through the mirror. "Do you remember how it looked before?"

"No." I lied. Gheesh, he had a big ego.

He pursed his lips and studied me. I'm sure he knew I was lying. I wondered if he would call me out. "Guess I'm not that memorable," was his reply.

I lifted one shoulder in a half shrug. The gum in my mouth felt like a piece of cement all of the sudden and my jaw ached every time I chewed. I stepped around the chair and reached for a tissue, discreetly spitting out the gum and throwing it away. Then I reached for the clippers and plugged them in, resting then in front of the mirror.

"Short on the sides, a little longer on the top," he instructed.

I grabbed a clean black comb and my sheers and took my place behind the chair.

One, two, three… I counted and then pushed my fingers into his hair.

It was soft and a little unruly. It was thick so it instantly covered my hands, hiding them from sight.

I hope I can't find them. The thought made me jerk and the tip of the sheers caught on his hair and pulled.

"Sorry," I said, clearing my throat, and pulled my hands away.

After that I tried not to think about who was sitting here. I tried to only focus on the hair.

That lasted about five seconds. How was a girl supposed to be so close to a man who literally made her heart race and not be affected?

After I combed the hair and checked its length, I decided to remove some of the bulk with the scissors. "I'm going to cut your hair dry today," I told him. "Using the clippers on wet hair doesn't work that well."

"Do your thing," he drawled.

I ignored the little flippy feeling in my stomach and got to work, removing some of the shagginess at the base of his neck and around his ears. He smelled so good that it was almost distracting. A clean scent with a hint of spice. It was an older scent, one that had been around for a long time, but it was my favorite. *Old Spice.* It was all man and it taunted my senses as I worked.

He didn't speak when I set down the scissors and picked up the clippers and snapped on one of the guards. I spun his chair around so our backs were to the mirror, and I breathed a sigh of relief. His eyes were so gorgeous and I had felt them on me the whole time I worked.

I moved quickly and confidently, trimming the hair close to the base of his neck and up around his ears. I did a low, gradual fade to the top, leaving it long and not quite faded all the way. I would clean it all up with the sheers.

After I was done with the clippers, I spun him back around and our eyes collided in the mirror. His new shorter hair drew attention to his square jaw and the stubble that grew there. When we went out, he was clean-shaven.

In fact, he seemed a little worn all around. He was still sexy as hell, but there was something about him that seemed… tired.

Before I knew what I was doing, I was asking him about himself. "How have you been?"

"Busy."

Too busy to call, I thought bitterly.

"How about you?"

"Fine," I said, giving the same generic answer I always gave when someone asked me about myself.

As I cut the top of his hair, I leaned into him. Every so often I would brush up against the side of his arm or his shoulder. My body tingled with awareness and never before had I ever felt like cutting someone's hair was so… intimate.

I stepped around to the front and leaned over him, trying to reach the hair, holding out my arms.

"Here," he said softly, spreading his knees apart and creating an opening to step between his legs.

I stepped closer, only because it made my job easier, and ran my fingers through his hair, pulling it up to look at it. A soft groan rumbled in his throat and I looked down.

"That feels good," he murmured, his eyes slipping closed.

Damn if that didn't make me want to do it again. The butterflies in my stomach were out of control, and I knew I was going to be tied up with fluttery energy all day, long after he was gone.

I kept cutting, running my hands through his tresses. He didn't groan again, but I couldn't help but notice the way his body relaxed into the seat. Poor guy, he must have been stressed.

I reminded myself not to feel sorry for him.

When I was done, I went around to the back and quickly checked the length all over, making sure it was even.

Then I ran my hands through it again, giving it a tousled look. "How's this?"

His eyes opened and he looked in the mirror. "Looks really good," he said, his eyelids slightly closed.

He wasn't looking at his hair.

He was looking at me.

We stood there for long, silent, charged seconds. It was the same kind of chemistry that sizzled between us the day we met and then again on our first and only date. Was I just imagining it? Did he not feel it too?

It was practically undeniable.

"So the, uh…" I said, my words getting lost in his gaze. "Uh, the haircut is to your liking?"

He finally glanced at his hair and nodded.

I made it. This was done. "Great," I said and set my tools down. I reached for the cape when he stopped me.

"Would you mind shampooing it? I have to go in to work later."

"Sure," I said, mentally dying. More touching him. With water. And soap.

It made me think of a shower with him. Naked. I jerked and then braced myself on the side of his chair. What the hell was I doing having these thoughts? I was at work!

"Right this way," I said, walking away and not looking to make sure he followed. I knew he was right behind me. My body was practically humming with his close proximity.

I led him to an open shampoo bowl and he sat down. I arranged the cape (figures the pink didn't make him look less manly) and then guided him back to rest his neck in the bowl. I turned the water on, testing it out on my hand until I got the desired temperature.

Slowly, I let the water cascade over his head. "Is that water okay?"

"Perfect," he murmured, his eyes slipping closed.

I wet his hair and then pumped some shampoo into my hand and massaged my fingers into his scalp. The scent wafted up around us and bubbles coated my fingers. I noted that he had goose bumps along his arms and it gave me some sort of pleasure to know it was my touch that did that to him.

I spent a little longer than I needed bent over him and washing his hair. And then I rinsed it with warm water and worked some conditioner through the ends (he didn't need it, but I sure had a good time). I couldn't help but give him a little scalp massage, and then I lifted his head to massage the back of his neck.

He heaved a great sigh and I noted the goose bumps on his skin remained the entire time.

After I was done I towel-dried his hair and directed him back to my station where I combed it, blasted it for a few seconds with the dryer, and then styled it so it was effortlessly messy.

"All done," I said, peeling away the pink cape and ignoring the feeling of regret because it was time for him to leave.

He sat there for long moments, looking at me like he wanted to say something, but then he got up. "Thanks," he said and then went toward the receptionist without a backward glance.

Clearly the chemistry I felt before had been my imagination.

I didn't look his way again; instead, I cleaned up the hair from the floor and put away my tools. I glanced at my watch. I still had a couple hours left before I could go home. I wished this day was over. I was ready to go home, eat a pint of ice cream, and wallow.

Wallow over one stinking date.

Yes, I was pathetic.

But it had been a really good date.

I had several minutes before my next client arrived so I focused on my reflection in the mirror. My blond hair was a little longer than chin length and it was styled in a messy little bob. Some of the strands flipped out around my face and I had side-swept bangs that drew attention to my blue eyes—not nearly as deep and blue as his were.

Part of me wondered if the color of his eyes was what inspired his name.

No thinking about him! I told myself and directed my attention back to the mirror. My cheeks were slightly flushed against my clear, creamy complexion, my nose was small and straight, and my full pink lips could use a little lip-gloss. I bent, fishing the gloss out of my bag, and when I stood back up, he was there.

"Blue," I gasped, pressing a hand to my chest.

"For you," he said, laying some folded bills on the station.

My heart thundered in my chest, and if I squeezed the gloss any tighter, it was going to explode. "Thanks," I murmured, breathless. Why was he standing so close?

He reached out and cupped his large, warm hand over my elbow and stepped a little closer. He brought his lips right up beside my ear.

"You're not so easy to forget," he whispered.

I sucked in a breath and my mouth ran dry. The room actually went a little blurry. I blinked, focusing on the spot where he stood.

But he was gone.

I stared at the door for a long time, his whispered words echoing through my head.

2

Blue

I received confirmation today. Confirmation that she was definitely pissed off at me. I hadn't been surprised by that. But I was surprised by the intensity of her anger. Even after all these weeks, she was still mad I never called.

That also confirmed something else.

She still wanted me.

The chemistry between us was undeniable. From the minute I stepped into that salon, she was all I could see. All I could feel.

She tried to act like she didn't care, like I was just some guy she met once. But she couldn't fool me. I caught the way she would look at me and then force away her eyes. The way she took extra care with her tools and scissors before getting started.

God, I could still smell her honeysuckle scent that practically wrapped around me every single time she leaned so close. Thank God for that stupid pink cape. It covered up the parts of me that had trouble hiding my strong and lusty reaction to her.

I'd been getting my hair cut all my life, but never, not one time had it ever given me a hard-on. I thought back to the way her perky, full breasts brushed against me when she sometimes moved. The way her black top clung to her narrow hips and her black and white skirt flirted with her ankles and hugged her tight ass. It made me itch to grab her, to pull her into my lap…

She looked as good as I remembered. Better, in fact. Her hair was golden blond with streaks of very light blond. The way it flipped out around her face drove me crazy. It was like she walked around with permanent bedhead, and all I could think about was what she would look like spread out across my sheets.

Her lips were full and ripe, like a juicy peach, and her blue-gray eyes were muted like the sky on a cloudy day. She seemed smaller than I remembered, though she wasn't wearing high-heeled boots like the time I took her out. Right before I left, I actually had to lean down to whisper in her ear, and it made me want to curl around her protectively.

But she didn't need protection. Julie was a girl with a set of claws on her. I noted today that they were painted a very eye-catching pink. I wondered how much work it was going to be to get her to retract those claws.

Would it even be worth the headache I knew she would cause me?

Maybe I should let it go, chalk it up to bad timing, and ask someone else out.

Even as I thought it, my body revolted against the thought. Yeah, I could ask someone else out, but it wouldn't be the one I really wanted. I had spent weeks, months even, thinking about her, drawing up her face and the sound of her laugh whenever life got too dark or too stressful for me to deal. Without even knowing it, she'd quickly and irrevocably became the place my mind drifted whenever I needed some sort of comfort.

Even her spiteful and sarcastic behavior today wouldn't change that. If anything, it endeared her to me more.

I shook my head. *Blue, a high-maintenance woman is the last thing you need.*

Still, the thought of driving her to the brink of madness and then kissing her back had an intense appeal to me. Life with someone like Julie would definitely not be boring. She would likely drive me insane, make me curse, and torture me in ways no other woman would.

What was wrong with me that made me want to move closer instead of farther away?

It's just stress. It's just you getting back to reality, I told myself. My job, my work life was full of drama. My home life needed to be calmer, more steady.

I sighed and took another wrong turn. I kept turning and driving in all different directions just to be sure that I wasn't being followed. I wasn't. I was told that I was safe. I liked to take precautions.

'Course, I already knew it was safe. If I hadn't been sure, I wouldn't have gone to her to get a haircut.

I guess some habits are hard to break.

I sighed when the station came into sight. I slowed and pulled into the lot, grabbing my duffle out of the back and jogging to the entrance.

What I needed to do was get back into the swing of things. Focus on the job. Always the job.

But it wasn't the job that I kept thinking about.

It was her.

3

Julie

My last client of the day was a walk-in. Technically, my day was done, but she was here and I was free so I extended my hours. I was exhausted. Seeing Blue again had pretty much made me feel like I had a gigantic shot of adrenaline straight to the heart, and when it drained away, I was left feeling like a wobbly noodle.

The woman in my chair was probably at least seventy years old. She had short curly hair, a rounded figure, and light wrinkles on her pale cheeks. Her eyes were bright and kind and she smiled a lot, which is probably the reason I offered to stay.

She leaned her cane against my workstation— which was a white built-in against the wall, with drawers and cubbies reaching to almost the ceiling on each side of the large rectangular mirror. There were bright lights overhead and in front of the mirror was a bar that ran across that held my blow dryer and styling tools.

She lowered herself down into the black chair, and I pulled out the black cape (okay, so maybe I *didn't* spill something on it) and draped it around her shoulders.

I pumped the chair up with my foot, bringing her to the correct height for me to work. "What can I do today for you, hon?"

The woman's hands moved around underneath the cape, and I watched as she drew out a folded-up section of a magazine. She'd brought a picture. I liked when clients brought a picture because it gave me an exact idea of what they were looking for so I didn't have to try to interpret what they tried to tell me.

"I want to look like this," she said and unfolded the paper and held it out to me.

It was Halle Berry.

I looked at her and then back at the paper. I tilted my head. I squinted my eyes. I shut one eye and looked at her that way.

Yeah, it was just as I thought.

Hopeless.

I sighed. "Hon," I began, trying to be sweet as I could. "I can absolutely cut your hair this way." It was the cut that Halle had made famous around the world. The ultra-short one with tasseled layers at the top. "But you do know that even if I cut your hair like this, you're not going to look like Halle Berry?"

Why must people always think they need to look like a celebrity? The good thing about people and hair was that you had the immense opportunity to define your own style, to be creative. Why look like someone else when you could look like you?

She laughed. "Oh, dear, yes, I know that." She smiled and pointed. "But I do love that cut. I was thinking it would be easy to get ready for church on Sundays."

I nodded. "Well, it definitely would." I placed the picture on the table nearby and ran my hands through her hair. It was surprisingly thick and well bodied. "How about this," I suggested, leaning down beside her ear and looking at her through the mirror. "Let's get some honey-blond highlights in there and really make it pop. Then I'll cut it just like that and show you how to style it."

"Blond?" she asked, looking over her grayish hue.

I nodded encouragingly. "Honey, you will give Halle a run for her money!"

She smiled ruefully. "Let's do it."

A little over an hour later, she stepped out of the Razor's Edge looking like a million bucks. Judging from the bounce in her step, I would say she felt like one hot lady.

I sighed. All in a day's work.

I carried the empty bowl of coloring mix back into the little kitchen and rinsed it out in the sink. Then I gave it a light wash, cleaning the highlighting brush out as well and placed them on the drying rack to dry overnight.

"Julie," Sandra said, entering the little room behind me.

I turned from the staff fridge where I was reaching in to grab my empty water thermos and my polka dotted reusable lunch bag.

"Yes?" I asked, mentally going over my station to make sure I hadn't left anything lying about.

Sandra was the owner and top stylist of the Razor's Edge Salon. She was the queen bee around here. She employed all the staff and paid us all an hourly rate. We were allowed to keep all the tips we made and didn't have to split them. We also received a percentage of commission from the designer line of hair care products we sold in the salon.

She was a nice woman, but she was slightly intimidating. She was very business oriented, which I respected, but sometimes her anal ways gave me a stomach ache.

"I saw that woman's hair," she began, leaning in the doorway and crossing her arms over her white blouse. "It looked stunning."

Relief washed through me. "Oh, thank you. I thought it looked great too."

She nodded, approval in her eyes. "Your talent has really grown in the last year," she said.

"I really appreciate you noticing and saying so, Sandra."

She nodded. "Of course. When my stylists do well, so does my salon. Every client that walks out of here is like a walking advertisement. You make us look good."

The compliment made me feel good.

"I was wondering if perhaps you might be open to more responsibilities around here?"

I hadn't expected that. Not at all. "What about the senior girls?" There were lots of stylists who had been here much longer than me and they were great.

"You have the youth and young image I would like to represent the salon."

Wow. I was flattered. "That would be wonderful."

Sandra smiled. "Great! Maybe we can meet tomorrow after your shift and sit down in my office to discuss the details?"

I agreed and then she disappeared. I grabbed my water and lunch bag and returned to my station to make sure it was tidy, grabbed my oversized leather purse, and headed out into the parking lot.

I checked my cell and I had a couple texts from my bestie Dee.

Where are you?
Sorry. Running late. B there soon.
I'm starving.
Eat without me.
No!
I smiled at my phone. **Order for me?**
Will do.

I smiled. I'm sure she would enjoy ordering me all her favorites so she could eat half my plate.

I climbed in my Hyundai and drove toward the Applebee's where I was meeting Dee. The parking lot was full and it took a minute to find a place to park. I hurried inside, stopping at the bathroom to wash my hands, and then found Dee sitting in a booth near one of the windows.

"Thanks," I said, slipping into the booth and taking a sip of the Diet Coke that was waiting for me.

"Food should be here soon," she said, tucking her smart phone into her purse and looking up.

"What did you get me?"

"Oh, the usual. A big hamburger and fries."

I rolled my eyes. There was no way she ordered me a cow on a plate. I was a vegetarian. "Care to try again?"

She sighed. "I ordered you that pasta dish with the veggies in it."

My stomach growled appreciatively. "Yum."

"I ordered a cow so try and hold back your gag when it gets here. I'm starving."

It didn't bother me to watch other people eat meat. I just didn't like the taste and texture of it. I hadn't always been a vegetarian. I just felt much better when I didn't have a pound of rotting meat in my gut. (Fun fact: meat can take up to two weeks to make its way out of the human body. If you ask me, it's the reason so many guys fart and stink. All that meat rotting in there.)

"So what's been going on?" I asked my friend.

"You know, the usual. Threatening Craig about leaving the toilet seat up, throwing his laundry all over the place, and never refilling the toilet paper roll when it's empty."

I laughed. "Sounds like living together is all you dreamed it would be."

She snorted and took a drink of her bright-green martini. "He's driving me nuts, Jules."

I patted her hand. "You two will get used to being together twenty-four-seven."

"Speaking of boyfriends…" she began.

I groaned and started digging through my bag, mining out the tips I made that day and putting them together so I could stick them in my wallet.

"There's this friend of Craig's—"

"No," I said, effectively cutting her off. "Don't even think about it. I am not going out on a blind date."

"I've seen him. It isn't blind."

"No."

She sighed.

The waitress arrived with our food. I practically drooled just looking at it. I dug into the pasta as soon as the waitress walked away. It was warm and creamy. So good.

"Seriously," Dee said. "You can't just ignore dating."

"I'm not."

She snorted.

"That is very unladylike," I informed her.

She waved her fork at me (why she needed a fork to eat a burger I would never know). "Don't try to change the subject."

I gave up and shoved a huge bite in my mouth, glancing down, and I finally realized I still had a wad of cash in my lap. I took a quick sip of soda and then unfolded the bills to flatten them out.

A business card fluttered from between the bills and just missed my bowl of goodness.

"What's that?" Dee said, her eyes narrowing on the card.

I caught the symbol for the local Jacksonville PD and the bottom fell out of my stomach. Had Blue actually slipped me his card with my tip?

"Nothing," I said and reached to grab it.

She had the reflexes of a ballerina on speed and snatched it away before my hand even thought about grabbing it and shoving it under my butt (no one would look there).

She gasped, the fry in her fingers falling from her grasp.

Here we go.

Her eyes were huge, like a bug. She looked at me and the card. "Is this *him*?" she whisper yelled.

The women in the booth nearby gave us a curious glance.

"Who?" I played dumb.

Her eyes narrowed. "You know exactly. Judging from the quick blush to your cheeks and the way your eyes are darting around, I would have to say that is a big fat yes."

"Geez, are you a private eye when I'm not looking?"

She looked smug, but it quickly melted into a look of pity. "Julie," she said empathetically. "It was one date. You have to move on."

Wait for it…

We said it at the same time. I couldn't help it. "Sweetie. He's just not that into you."

She scowled.

"Fine." She sniffed. "Make fun. I'm only trying to help my best friend who is carrying around the card of a man who never called and turning down perfectly good blind dates."

I groaned. "Please. You know damn well that Mr. Blind Date is probably at home right now with his mom and his twenty cats, knitting them each a sweater for Christmas."

Dee laughed. "You set a girl up with one weirdo…" she said dejectedly.

It was the weirdo to end all weirdoes. I shuddered. "I haven't been carrying that card around," I admitted.

Her interest perked.

"I saw him. Today."

"I need every detail. Now." She leaned over the table like I was about to divulge the whereabouts of some priceless treasure.

"He came in for a haircut. I cut his hair. He left. The end."

"Did you stab him?"

I giggled. "Thought about it."

"Did you at least knick him?"

I shook my head. Truth was the minute I touched him, I couldn't imagine doing any kind of bodily harm to him. It wouldn't just hurt him, but me too.

I was a head case.

I reached across the table and grabbed up Dee's martini and took a swig. The liquor burned my throat the whole way down. My eyes watered. I was such a lightweight. That one sip would likely make me tipsy.

"Did he ask you out?"

I shook my head. "No. He didn't even act like he was interested. He probably didn't realize his card was stuck in the bills."

"Maybe he wants you to call him." Dee suggested.

We both looked at each other and laughed. Then we laughed some more. I didn't call guys. I was a little old-fashioned like that. I wanted to be approached by a man. I wanted him to make the first move. I also thought the guy should pay for the date. Yeah, I know. It's the new millennium. Feminism is strong— Go Women! But there's something to be said for some chivalry now and then. I wasn't about to swoon for some guy who thinks I can open my own door and pay for his dinner.

Nope.

Being in a relationship is a whole other ballgame… Then I believe in equal opportunity for all. But in the first steps of dating, I think the man should take the lead.

"It doesn't matter," I said, taking another bite. "He's not interested and I'm not calling." I grabbed up the money and the card and shoved it to the very bottom of my bag.

I could leave it on the table. I could take it and throw it away.

I couldn't bring myself to do it.

4

Blue

Two weeks later, I found myself in need of another haircut.

A man in my profession had to look clean-cut and respectable. At least that's what I told myself as I was sitting in my steel-gray Dodge Challenger, staring at the salon from behind my windshield.

Never mind the fact the first haircut I had in months was two weeks ago. That was different. And this time I had extra motivation.

"Shit," I muttered under my breath as I shut off the engine, climbed out of the car, and slammed the door. Two weeks of throwing myself back into work. Two weeks of focusing on the job.

Only my focus was jack.

Every time I thought I had a good day, I would spend the nights in my apartment daydreaming. About a blonde I had no business thinking about.

I walked up the steps of the salon and went inside. The place was pretty ritzy. 'Course, what did I know? My mom was the one who usually cut my hair, in the center of her dining room, with an old towel wrapped around my shoulders. It was free. She'd been cutting it since I was a boy, so why change it if it wasn't broken?

The floors were made of light-colored Travertine tile. There was a mosaic fountain by the front door and the trickling water blended with the Zen-type music that played through speakers in the ceiling.

The receptionist desk was round with a young brunette sitting in the center. The top of the desk was black granite and there was a large, very organized display of hair products to the left.

I had no idea so many different bottles of stuff existed.

To the right of the desk was a long row of stylist chairs lining the wall. All of them had built-in white cabinetry, bright lights, and black stylist chairs. The mirrors bounced light around the room and the hum of women's voices and blow-dryers filled the air.

Toward the very back of the room were several stations of people getting their nails done, something I never planned to do. Just being in this place to get my hair cut was a danger to my man card.

The guys at the station would have a field day if they could see me now.

The receptionist perked up as soon as her eyes landed on me, so I smiled and stepped forward. "Is Julie available for a haircut?" I asked, glancing in Julie's direction.

She was cutting someone's hair and laughing. The sound caused something in me to tighten. I replayed that laugh over in my head so many times in the past few weeks, but nothing I ever heard in my head sounded near as good as the live thing.

"Julie is with a client," the receptionist said. "But Layla has an opening."

The girl I presumed was Layla came forward, long, dark hair swinging around her shoulders. She was pretty hot. Her lips were red and she wore impressive high heels accentuating her mile-long legs.

I considered my options. Accepting and letting Layla cut my hair would probably be a smart move. I told myself I wouldn't come here anyway, yet here I stood. My eyes drifted over to Julie. She was no longer paying attention to the client in her chair but was watching me.

Layla stepped closer and put a hand on my arm. "Ready?"

Something passed behind Julie's eyes… something that looked suspiciously like disappointment. Then she turned back to what she was doing.

"I'll wait for Julie," I said.

Layla's eyes widened in surprise. I flashed her a grin. "Nothing personal. Maybe next time."

She smiled and grabbed a card off the reception desk and held it out. "Here's my card. It has my number on it. If you ever want to make an appointment… or go out for drinks."

Any other time I would have been all over this girl. I would have asked her out on the spot. But today I had no interest. Today, the back of my neck itched because I felt the subdued gray-blue-eyed stare I knew was behind me.

I forced a smile toward Layla and pocketed the card, giving her a little wink. "Thanks. Maybe I'll take you up on that."

Yeah, it was a lie. But I wasn't about to hurt her feelings.

She gave me a smile and then moved away, shaking her hips as she went. I watched… because I was a guy. And because it was a nice view.

I took a seat near the reception desk, looking at all the girly magazines and products around me. Man, I must really have it bad to subject myself to a place like this.

Thankfully, I didn't have to wait long. Julie escorted her client to the reception desk and gave her a warm smile while she helped her schedule another appointment for a future date. I couldn't help but watch her.

There was something sincere about her. Something that drew my eyes like she was standing under a spotlight that only I could see. Her bangs were falling over one eye and every once in a while she would push at them while she talked. It was a move I found oddly endearing.

Once the client was gone, Julie turned her eyes toward me. I noticed her smile lost a little bit of its authenticity. I didn't like that. Not at all.

"Blue," she said, coming over to stand before me.

I stood up. "Got time for a haircut?"

Her eyes raked over my face and then to my hair. Her body was slightly tense, and I prepared myself for a no.

"Yeah," she said. "Come on back."

I let out the breath I'd been holding and followed her to her station. She was wearing a pair of white jeans that hugged her ass like a glove. Her black and white shirt had wide horizontal stripes on it, was fitted, and hugged her back and narrow waist.

When she turned and gestured to the chair, I noticed the necklace hanging low around her neck. It was a giant red heart that hung crooked. Her hair was its usual "just been laid" look and for once it made me a little mad instead of turned on.

I didn't want to think about her getting her hair messed up like that by anyone but me.

I needed a beer. While I was watching sports. This damn girly fru-fru place was starting to get to me.

"Just trimming you up today?" Julie said, pulling out a black cape to drape around my shoulders.

I took it as a good sign she wasn't going to try to torture me with the pink one today.

"Yeah."

"I'll do like last time and trim it up. Then I'll shampoo it for you." When her hands delved into my hair and rubbed against my scalp, little goose bumps broke out over my arms.

"You have really good hair," she murmured.

"So do you."

The compliment seemed to make her mad, and she pulled her hands away to reach for her tools. Why did women have to be so damn complicated all the time?

She used the clippers on the side, shortening it up a bit and then cleaning up the neck area. Then she used the scissors to trim the top. As she worked, the only sound between us was the light snipping of the sheers.

"So I never apologized for not calling after our date."

Her movements paused. Her eyes darted to me in the mirror and then quickly away. She used the black comb to pull up a section of hair and began cutting again. "No big deal," she replied nonchalantly.

"I wanted to."

She snorted. It made me smile.

"Things at work got crazy. I had to go out of town."

She looked at me again. "You did?"

I nodded. "Yeah. I was gone for a while."

"I hope everything's okay."

"It's fine."

She set down the scissors and ran her fingers through my hair again. I had to work to keep my eyes open.

"All done," she said, patting me on the shoulder. "Let's get you shampooed."

Damn. That was fast. Dutifully, I followed her back to the shampoo bowl and sat down. The water was warm, the shampoo smelled pretty good… and her hands… Damn, I loved having her hands on me.

Once again, I was happy this cape was so long.

This time after she blow-dried it, she put a little something on her fingers and rubbed them together. Her movements were quick and sure when she styled it, and then she stepped aside for me to see. The front was tousled and sticking up a little.

She gave me the "just been laid" look.

An image of me shoving her up against the mirror and burying my tongue in her mouth flashed through my head. It was so strong and so wanted that my hands clenched into fists in my lap.

"I did something a little different," she said, looking a little unsure.

"I like it," I said, noting the hoarseness in my tone.

She smiled. A genuine smile.

Do it again.

Her smile fell away and it appeared she was having some kind of inner debate. Whatever it was went quickly because she sighed and the grabbed up the bright-green container of what she put in my hair and held it out. "Here, this is what I used. You can take it."

"You're giving this to me?"

She bit her bottom lip (which drove me crazy) and nodded. "You can use it to make your hair look like that."

I looked at the product clutched in her hand and then up at her face. "Have dinner with me."

She jerked like I slapped her. That wasn't really the reaction I was hoping for.

"What?"

"Dinner. Tonight. With me."

Her eyes narrowed. "I thought you weren't interested."

I laughed. "Do you think I would subject myself to this place if I wasn't?"

She crossed her arms over her chest. "You could always ask Layla."

"I already asked you."

She shoved the hair stuff in my hand and then picked up a broom and dust pan. Her movements were stiff as she cleaned up what little hair she cut off me. "You had your chance. You never called."

I grabbed her by the elbow and spun her around. "You had a good time."

"You have a big ego."

I moved quickly, crowding her personal space. "Are you saying you didn't? Are you saying you don't feel the chemistry between us?"

"Maybe I already have a boyfriend," she replied, jerking her arm out of my grasp.

Actually, I hadn't thought of that. Because I couldn't think of her as anything but mine. Something sour rose up in my gut. "Do you?"

She sniffed.

A slow grin spread out over my face. "I'll pick you up at seven." I dug some money out of my pocket and put it beside the mirror. "Keep the change."

Then I walked out of the salon without looking back.

5

Julie

When I got up this morning I really didn't expect for my day to go as follows:

—Spill coffee on my shirt and have to change.

—Deal with three clients who have unrealistic expectations about the hair attached to their head.

—Watch Layla hit on Blue. Watch him turn her down.

—Watch Blue ask me out.

—Agree.

—Walk around in giddy shock and then be called into my boss' office for a meeting I forgot about.

I couldn't even be nervous. I was already so tied up in knots about my dinner with Blue that everything else seemed like details.

"Julie, please sit down," Sandra said, in a smooth, southern voice.

I moved around the chair and sat down.

"You've been doing a great job the last couple weeks with the scheduling of the stylists and dealing with the product placements."

"Thank you." I actually enjoyed it. It meant a little bit longer hours, but that extra pay was nice and I took pride in the displays around here. I think the way I had it set up actually increased sales. The scheduling was a bit tricky because a few of the stylists thought they could take advantage of me by requesting certain days and shifts, but I quickly let them know it wasn't going to happen. I planned to treat everyone fairly around here.

"I was wondering if you would be willing to take on the inventory."

"Inventory?"

Sandra nodded. "Yes, since you're handling product placement, I figured giving you access to the suppliers and catalogues would be a good idea. You are welcome to bring in any new lines you think would sell well. Just keep in mind I only want to carry three or four lines at a time. Anything beyond that—"

"Will just look cluttered and inconsistent." I finished.

She looked impressed.

"I agree. Keeping the lines to a minimum will give the impression that we only carry the best and pay attention to what the clients need."

"Yes. Exactly. But we will always carry Paul Mitchell. You can change the others, just not that one. Paul is a friend of mine."

She was friends with *Paul Mitchell?* He was like the hair care king.

I agreed and she continued on. "You will need to set aside a block of time every week to take stock and keep track of what's selling and what we need more of. Since you're handling the products, I'd like you to go ahead and handle the color as well."

I nodded, thinking of the cabinets full of hair coloring products in the back.

"Those will need reordered more than the products out front."

"Okay."

"I will show you how to handle the stock and then you can take over next week."

I followed her back into the little kitchen where the staff kept their lunch and salon supplies. She quickly but thoroughly went through the way to keep track, told me what usually got used up the fastest (the blond colors), and then handed me a notebook and a binder with all the supplier information.

My eyes kept straying to a door that led off the kitchen, a door I'd never gone behind.

"Sandra?" I asked. "What's in there?"

"Oh, that's just a closet. The water heater and the electrical box."

Boring.

We finished up the meeting and then I gathered up my stuff and hurried to my car. I had a date tonight!

Before climbing into my Hyundai, I sent off a quick text to Dee.

Have a Date. Meet me at my place. Wardrobe 9-1-1.

I didn't wait for a reply. I just shoved my phone in my bag and headed for my townhouse just a few miles away.

I lived off of Gumbranch Road in a little development of townhouses that were only several years old. They were in rows. Each of them looked the same with light-colored vinyl siding, dark shutters, and concrete steps leading off the sidewalk and up to the front door.

I parked in my spot in front of my house and walked past the pots of colorful fall mums lining my steps and let myself inside.

The quiet of the home wrapped around me and I sighed. The scent of vanilla cinnamon wafted through the air from the wax melter that I always had on, and I dumped my bag and keys on the little glass-topped table by the door.

I kicked off my shoes and walked through the cozy living room and into the kitchen, which was in the back of the house. The slate tiles were cool against my bare feet, and I went straight toward the dark wood cabinet and pulled down my favorite mug and filled it with water. Once it was heating in the microwave, I rummaged around for a teabag and then leaned against the counter (it wasn't granite, but it was made to look like it) and waited.

The kitchen was my favorite room in the house, with slate floors, dark cabinets, and black appliances. There was a small island in the center that had a butcher block top and wheels on the bottom. The base of the island I painted a deep plum color, and it had a shelf where I kept some pots and kitchen items stacked neatly.

Against the wall was a single French door that led out onto a private covered patio. Well, the realtor called it private, but my neighbors had one just like it on either side, so if they were out at the same time I was, there really wasn't any privacy.

The microwave dinged and I pulled out the steaming mug, dunked the teabag inside, and added a generous dollop of honey. The first sip of hot tea was always the best.

I sighed as the warm sweetness traveled down my throat. I took my mug and left the kitchen, going back out into the living room, and headed to the stairs. Just as my foot hit the bottom step, the doorbell rang frantically.

I laughed and pulled it open. "That was fast," I said as Dee pushed her way inside.

"Are you kidding!? You said the word date. I broke every speed law to get over here."

"Don't let Blue hear you say that."

Her jaw fell open. "Blue asked you out."

"Yep."

"You said yes?"

I paused. Okay, I probably shouldn't have. But I couldn't resist him.

"Ohmigod," Dee said, her words running together as she dragged me upstairs and into my bedroom.

I sat my mug on the white bedside table and flopped down on the fluffy down comforter on my bed.

"How did this happen?" Dee said, pacing. Then she gasped. "Did you call him?"

"No!" I shot out. This girl has some pride, you know.

"He came to you?"

I told her about his second visit to the salon. She didn't say anything but raced through my bathroom and into the walk-in closet. "Girl, you need to look hot, as in H-A-W-T. Make him eat his heart out."

Sounded good to me. Giving him a taste of what he does to me wasn't a bad idea.

I fell back into my hundreds of pillows (okay, it was more like ten) and thought about the first—and last—date I had with Blue. North Carolina had been on the cusp of summer. The weather was in that special in-between state that we southerners never got enough of. It wasn't too hot and it wasn't too cold. It was warm and when the breeze blew, there was just a hint of chill in the air.

He picked me up and drove us to Wilmington, which was about an hour south of Jacksonville. We ended up at the Mayfaire Shops at Brixx, this totally delicious wood-fired pizza place. We sat outside underneath their awning and ate wood-fired pizza and sampled some of their brewed beers.

We laughed a lot. I remembered thinking about how laidback and relaxed he was, considering the profession he worked in afforded so much authority. In fact, if I hadn't known he was a police officer, it would have been the last thing I would have guessed about him.

After dinner, we walked around the outdoor shops, not really paying attention to anything because we were so wrapped up in each other. When it started to thunder, he pulled me into the nearby movie theater and bought tickets to a movie I barely remembered. Who could pay attention to the big screen when someone that literally made my heart race was sitting just beside me? During those blissful two hours, I practically lived for those casual touches when his arm would brush against mine or when our fingers would bump together when we both reached for the popcorn at the same time.

My entire body had been hyper aware of him the entire time. When the movie was almost over, he reached over and threaded his fingers through mine. I'd never felt such a nest of butterflies inside my body than I had right then. He left our hands joined together, resting them in my lap until the credits rolled onto the screen.

It was storming when we walked out of the theater. Big, fat drops of rain that splashed in the huge fountain on the sidewalk as it lit up in flashes of blue and pink. We started to run for it, but then he pulled me back, keeping us in the pounding rain as he pulled a penny out his pocket and told me to make a wish.

I wished for him.

He tossed the penny in the fountain and then pulled me close.

I prayed to God he would kiss me.

I barely even noticed the rain at that point. All I felt was the beating of both our hearts against our chests. He lowered his head… but he didn't kiss me. Instead, he pressed his forehead against mine and started to dance.

We slow danced in the rain beside the color-changing fountain until both of us were soaked through.

Then he drove me home in his sexy car and walked me to the door like a gentleman. I anticipated his kiss… I craved it. I wanted it so desperately that when he left me on the steps without so much as a peck, I thought I might die. I even considered chasing him down and beating him with my purse.

Even the sharp disappointment of no kiss could fully erase the feeling, the giddiness of being in his arms while we danced.

And then I waited for him to call.

I stared at the phone. I checked it to make sure it was working when it never rang. I watched the door of the salon and my heart sped up when someone of his size and build walked in. But he never came. He never called.

It hurt way more than I thought it would.

It seemed stupid to get so twisted up after only a single date. Even knowing how stupid I was didn't stop me. As the weeks wore on, the weather heated up. I knew he would never call. It almost seemed impossible he hadn't felt what I had that night.

How one man could completely disregard me and still make it impossible for me to want to date anyone else I would never understand.

And now he was back.

Was he going to do this to me all over again?

What was that saying? *Fool me once, shame on you. Fool me twice, shame on me.*

"Earth to Julie," Dee yelled, cutting into my deep thoughts.

I lifted my head and looked at her. "Yeah?"

"Geez. You are completely tipsy."

"No, I'm not." I protested, pushing up into a sitting position.

She snorted. "Uh, yeah. You are. The only time you ever seem to stop listening is when you've had one too many to drink."

"I'm drinking tea."

"Apparently alcohol isn't the only thing that makes you tipsy. Blue does too."

I rolled my eyes. You couldn't get tipsy on a person. "What did you pick out?" I asked, changing the subject.

She held up a pair of dark skinny jeans and a low-cut purple top.

"With the tall black boots and black leather jacket?" I asked, tilting my head.

She smiled. "Now you're talking."

We chatted a little longer and then Dee left after making me promise to call her when I got home, no matter the time.

I took my time in the shower, shaving my legs (hey, a girl never wants to get caught looking like sasquatch) and doing my hair. I gave it a little extra mess because I was feeling edgy and nervous.

I was downstairs waiting at seven.

At seven fifteen, I checked my phone.

At seven forty-five, I wondered if I had imagined him asking me out.

At eight, I knew he wasn't coming.

There was surprise in Dee's voice when she answered the phone. "If you're calling me from a date, then I know it's not going well."

"He didn't show."

There was a very long pause on the other end of the line.

"Dee?"

"He's a dog. I'm plotting his murder. I need silence."

I laughed. Some of the sickness in my stomach loosened. I couldn't believe I fell for his charm again.

Shame on me.

I heard Dee's muffled voice. She was talking to someone in the background. Most likely it was Craig.

Then she came back on the line, loud and clear.
"We're going out."

"I don't think so," I protested. All I wanted to do was put on my ugly sweatpants and eat ice cream.

"Arguing is futile." She insisted. "We're going. We'll pick you up so you can drink."

"Fine," I muttered and hung up the phone.

A drink sounded like a pretty good idea right now.

6

Blue

This time I wasn't going to screw this up. With a woman like Julie, a guy didn't get many chances. Hell, I was surprised she gave me a second chance. But she had. And I wasn't going to waste it.

She didn't seem like the kind of girl who needed a lot to be impressed. Julie struck me as the kind of girl who wanted to feel like she was all her man could see. All he wanted. She was the kind of girl who would rather be lavished with attention than money.

I could do that.

It might not always be easy, but I had a feeling she was worth it.

I figured we'd drive out to Topsail Island, have dinner at a place on the water, and then end up on the beach. I was going to kiss her. Not kissing her the first time we went out had been hard and it was a decision I regretted to this day. Not knowing what she tasted like haunted me.

I locked my apartment and jogged down the concrete steps when my phone went off in my pocket. I glanced at the screen: Work.

I answered it with, "I'm busy."

"Markson, this is Cramer. We have a situation. We need you to come in," said a gruff, no-nonsense voice into my ear.

I winced. Cramer was like the boss of my boss. When he called, I came. Damn. "I'm actually on my way out," I tried.

"Good. I'll see you in a few."

Clearly the guy didn't know how to take a hint. I pointed the Challenger in the direction of the JPD and prayed this was some kind of situation that required five minutes. I was early to pick up Julie so I had a little bit of time to get this taken care of.

I strode into the station and swiftly made my way back to the police chief's office. I didn't bother to knock. They called. I came.

Chief Watson was bent over his desk with Cramer, and I got my first inkling that something big was up.

"Have a seat, Markson," Chief Watson instructed when he noticed me hovering in the door.

I sat down even though I felt like pacing the room. This reminded me of the last time I got called into his office. It ended with me falling off the face of the earth for months.

"We need you to go under again," Watson said, getting right to the point.

My stomach clenched. I sat there stiffly for the span of two heartbeats. "Same case?"

"Yes."

I exhaled. I always knew there was a possibility I would have to go back, but I really didn't think it would be so soon… if at all. "Was there a break in the case?"

Cramer spoke up for the first time since I walked in and sat down. "The department has learned some new information. Apparently, the supply of drugs pumping into the Myrtle Beach area has been followed back to this area."

That was surprising. Months ago I was called into the station unexpectedly and was told I was needed undercover on the outskirts of Myrtle Beach, South Carolina. Because the area is such a hotspot for entertainment and clubs, the drug scene was growing rapidly and new cocktails of dangerous drug combinations were appearing and claiming lives.

I was pulled from the unit here and sent deep undercover with a background story and a new ID to try to ascertain where the drugs were coming from, who was funneling them in, and to gain leads on how to stop the poisoning of a well-known vacation hotspot.

I was gone for months. Months of living in the ghetto. Months of no contact with my family. My friends. My life. I literally walked in the station one night a cop living his life and stepped out hours later with a new identity and strict orders to speak to no one that could possibly identify who I really was.

It had been the night I had my first and only date with Julie.

And now it was happening all over again.

I shook off the trip down memory lane and told myself I could wallow later. "So you're saying that someone here, in our town, is the cause of all the drug and violent activity down there?"

"It appears that way," Cramer confirmed.

A trail of expletives let loose from my mouth.

"My thoughts exactly, Markson," Watson muttered. "This is absolutely unacceptable. These punks are our on turf now. It's a direct challenge. We need to take them down."

"What do you want me to do?"

"We have it on good authority that some of the thugs that are connected to LeBraun in Myrtle Beach will be at a club tonight in Jacksonville. We want you to assume your former identity and go there. Accidentally bump into the crew and get in with them."

Concern rose up at back of my neck. "You're putting me undercover in the same town that I work and live in?"

Watson glanced at Cramer with a sour expression on his face. "It's not ideal. Under normal circumstances this would be a no-go. But we've been on this case for two years. This is the first break we've had at all."

That I believed. The reason I was pulled out after several months of work was because the case was going nowhere fast, and it was a waste to have so many guys working on it. "Can't you pull in someone from Myrtle?"

He shook his head. "We don't know who we can trust there. Some of the cops on the force are on the take. It's the same reason JPD was brought down there in the first place."

"Plus, some of the crew here might have come from down there," I murmured to myself.

"Exactly. You've been out of the loop here for months. You've just now been back to work and mostly it's been routine stuff. You're not in the club scene around here, are you?" he asked, a new apprising look coming into his eyes.

I shook my head. "Absolutely not." Clubs were not my thing, never had been.

He nodded, looking relieved. "You already know this case, details that new recruits wouldn't understand. We don't have to brief you on this stuff. Not only will your presence save us time, but frankly, you're our best option."

Cramer picked up where Watson left off. "Point blank, Markson, you're one of the youngest on the PD here, you fit the profile of a guy who might be in the drug business, and you've already built an identity that will open doors for us. We need you to do this."

I wasn't sure if I should be offended by what he said. It wasn't every day a guy was told that he looked like a drug dealer.

"I'll do it."

Watson clapped his hands with glee. "Good. From here on out, you don't come to the station. Don't call. Leave your personal possessions—your cell, your wallet, your car keys—everything on my desk. You'll get them back when the assignment is over."

Damn. I hated giving up my car. I loved that thing. But I couldn't run the risk of it being recognized. This was a fairly big town, but it wasn't so big that someone might not know the Challenger with the black racing stripe down the hood if they saw it.

"Don't go home. We've rented a new place where you'll be staying. It's been outfitted with clothes and food already. Here's the address." He handed me a slip that I glanced at only long enough to realize that the location was less than desirable.

"You're getting two cells. One for regular use; you can give the number to contacts. One that is only to be used to contact the station. Don't let them find the cell or you're screwed."

He droned on for what felt like hours, telling me stuff I already knew and outlining the "crew" of druggies that were in our area. I felt weary already. Dealing with these kinds of thugs was exhausting. You had to be on watch at all times. There was never a moment that I could let my guard down. One slipup could literally kill me or someone else.

When I couldn't sit another moment, I stood and paced to the office door. "Markson," Watson called, and I turned.

"I want these SOBs. They've been hiding right under our noses for too long. This is our town. If we let them get control of Jacksonville, they're going to take over the entire area from here all the way to Myrtle Beach."

"I'm on it."

He gave a brisk nod. "Their last victim was a thirteen-year-old on vacation. Died of a drug overdose. They're preying on kids now."

Fury radiated up from my bones. Punks who pick on kids made me sick. I might not have gotten these assholes last time, but this time… this time they were on my playing field. This time I had the upper hand.

"We have another officer from Raleigh down here working the case. He showed up about the same time we found out about the underground ring here.

His name is Slater. He's been informed about you. He'll be at the club tonight. He'll make some introductions."

Cramer handed me another slip of paper with the address and name of the club I was to go to tonight. It was one of the rowdiest in Jacksonville. Figured.

I committed the address to memory and then dropped it onto the desk. I couldn't take it with me. Then I committed my new address to memory and left that paper behind too. After I unloaded my pocket and keys, I noticed Watson watching me.

"There's some clothes in the back. Change. You don't look like a thug. Hell, you like you're going on a date."

"I was," I said, annoyance in my voice.

"They'll be plenty of time for dating later," Cramer said, clapping me on the back.

I wanted to laugh. This was the second time I'd screwed up with Julie. Sure, I might have dates in the future, but they sure as hell wouldn't be with her.

I glanced at the clock. It was already after eight.

Yep. All my chances with Julie went out the window over an hour ago when I stood her up.

7

Julie

"No way," I said when Craig turned into the parking lot of a club that I had only heard about but never been inside.

Dee peered at me from the darkened front seat of Craig's black Hummer. "Come on," she begged.

"Don't you know the reputation this place has?"

She shrugged. "I've heard it. But sitting at the bar at Chili's isn't going to help you forget about being stood up."

"Neither will you reminding me every five seconds," I snapped. Then I pressed my lips together. That was bitchy. "Dee—"

She held up her hand. "Save it. I know you're sorry. You gotta take your anger out on someone."

But not on my best friend.

"Look, this place is known for a good time. It's loud; it's busy. There's dancing. You need a couple shots and to shake it on the dance floor with some hottie."

There was something wrong with me. That didn't sound like fun at all. I thought longingly of my ice cream and sweatpants while Craig parked the Hummer in the nosebleed section where there weren't even any street lights. I decided to appeal to his manliness.

"You're going to let your girlfriend go into this bar? It could be dangerous."

He turned in the seat and looked at me. "So am I." Then he winked.

Clearly he wasn't going to be any help.

"Come on," Dee cajoled. "One drink. It'll be fun."

"Fine," I groaned. We were already here and I looked hot (if I do say so myself).

She squealed and we made our way across the parking lot, my heels teetering unsteadily against the layer of gravel coating the ground. The loud bass of the music thumped through the night air, practically vibrating the ground. The club was up ahead, a large, unassuming building. All the windows were dark— probably being blocked by some sort of covering or a coat of black paint. The entrance looked small compared to the vast empty walls. It was just a single door with one of those push bars across the front and a neon EXIT sign on the front.

As we approached, someone came out and the music grew even louder. Inside there was a bouncer at the door, taking money for the cover charge. Craig handed over some cash and we were invited inside by the grunting bouncer.

Classy.

The music was so loud I could barely hear myself think. The lighting was dim, most of it coming from flashing neon bulbs and a disco ball over the dance floor. There were booths lining the walls, all of them in the shadows, and a bar shoved up against the right side of the room.

It kind of looked like a huge empty gym. The walls were plain. The floor was wide-open for dancing in the center, and the bar was wooden with stools underneath.

There were people crowded everywhere— around the bar, around the booths, on the edges of the dance floor. The dance floor was seeing a lot of action as well. Couples and groups were gyrating and dancing all over the place. A DJ booth was set up on the far side of the room, and he was dancing it up to the tunes as well.

The air was thick in here, the amount of bodies making it overly warm. It smelled slightly of stale smoke and beer.

"Come on!" Dee yelled over the music and pulled me over to the bar. Craig pushed his way through the crowd and appeared several minutes later with a drink for each of us. He was also carrying a shot of clear liquid, which he extended to me.

I took it without question and swallowed it in one gulp. It burned the whole way down my throat, and I felt it coat my stomach with fiery warmth. I took a sip of the rum and coke in my hand and scanned the crowd.

"See anyone promising?" Dee asked, leaning into my ear. I rolled my eyes. In this place? Yeah right. I had a better chance of catching some weird airborne disease in here than I had of actually meeting a guy worth dating.

"No," I yelled. "I'm not looking anyway." The sting of being rejected by Blue again was still fresh. It was like one of those nasty cuts that just a brush of the air caused it to burn and sting fiercely. Unfortunately, I couldn't slap a Band-Aid over my entire body. I was going to have to deal.

I took another sip of the drink, feeling the effects of the shot already. I guess alcohol was sort of like my Band-Aid tonight. I never drank so I knew it wouldn't take much to take away the sting—if only for a little while.

A new song switched on, something by *Pink*, and suddenly I didn't mind it was so loud. I liked not having to think.

"Let's dance!" Dee said and pulled me out onto the dance floor.

The three of us found some space on the side and started moving to the beat. Dee was a good dancer. She ground herself against Craig, who used his hands to pull her a little closer. Eventually, I began to feel like the third wheel I was, and I shook my empty cup at her and pointed to the bar.

She nodded and I stepped off the floor and out of the crush of bodies. I tossed my cup in a nearby trashcan, not really intending to get another. I was already feeling it. I was a little fuzzy headed, my body was relaxed (relaxed = uncoordinated), and I knew if I drank any more I would be well on my way to drunk.

I wandered toward the bathroom, debating the toxicity of the germs in there, but my bladder made the decision for me. The alcohol was going right through me.

Halfway to the bathroom, someone stumbled into my path from a nearby booth. They bumped into me. "Sorry," they mumbled, righting themselves and disappearing into the crowd.

I adjusted my top and turned my head.

Familiar eyes collided with mine and my heart stopped. It literally stopped beating. I felt like every ounce of oxygen had been siphoned out of my lungs and they collapsed right there beneath my ribs.

Eyes that blue could only belong to one man.

My gaze raked over the rest of him, confirming what I already knew.

Blue was here.

He was wearing clothes I never would have guessed he owned. Scuffed-up jeans, a T-shirt, and a black leather jacket. On his head was a gray knit skull cap. It covered up the hair I ran my hands through just hours before. God, it felt like years.

Even more, there was a piercing in his lip, a tiny silver ring that the flashing lights above occasionally reflected off of.

It made me yearn to know what that metal felt like against my skin.

I shook my head. Standing here practically ogling how hot he looked was ridiculous.

I got stood up so he could come here and… and… Well, I don't know what he was doing. Except there was a blonde wearing a very tiny shirt cozied up to his side and looking at him like he was a steak and she hadn't eaten in weeks.

My eyes found his again, and I drew back in shock. I'd never seen such coldness in his eyes before. It was as if I was the last person on Earth he wanted to see.

His gaze flicked away, like he was dismissing me, and the girl at his side started kissing his neck. I was going to be sick.

I started moving again, rushing away from the table… from his angry stare. I didn't know what I could have possibly done to make him look at me like that. Hell, if anything, I should've been the one looking at *him* like that. He was the one that stood me up.

I pushed into the bathroom, no longer caring how filthy it was, and waited for a stall. I did my business (hovering over the toilet because I wasn't about to touch anything—okay, so I guess I *did* care about the germs after all) and then washing my hands at the sink. I glanced up in the mirror above and noted the slightly shell-shocked look on my face.

Pull yourself together, Julie, I told myself. *Go show him what he's missing.* I smirked at my reflection. How inconvenient for him that the girl he just stood up happened to be in the last place he expected.

After ruffling my hair a bit, I went back into the club, heading straight for the bar. I ordered another rum and coke and waved to Dee, who was still dancing it up on the floor with her man.

When my drink was ready, I pulled some cash out of my jeans, but a hand reached out to stop me. "I got this."

I watched as he threw some bills onto the counter, grabbed his beer, and turned to me.

He had very dark hair, almost black. It was wavy and a little too long, causing it to fall over his forehead and over one eye. He had smooth skin, brown eyes, and full lips. There was an arrogance that surrounded him, the kind that a guy carried when he thought he was God's gift to women.

He was totally not my type.

"Haven't seen you here before."

"There's a first time for everything." I had to say it so loud it didn't sound nearly as flirtatious as I planned.

Wait. I wanted to flirt?

I glanced down at the drink in my hand. Alcohol, a bruised heart, an angry ego, and the guy who caused it all just feet away was *not* a good combination.

He smiled, his eyes drifting over my body. I had to admit, it was nice someone seemed to notice how good I looked.

"Nice boots," he said, leaning in and speaking directly into my ear.

I didn't bother to reply. I just took a sip of my drink and watched as he pulled away. He was wearing jeans that rode low on his hips, a white wife-beater tank top, and a red button-up shirt (that wasn't buttoned).

Definitely not my type.

Of course, my type was the kind who stood girls up.

Maybe it was time for a new type.

"Let's dance," the guy said, sipping his beer and taking my hand.

"You got a name?" I yelled, following him to the dance floor.

"Dominick," he called. "People call me Dom."

He didn't ask my name. He didn't say anything. He just spun around to face me and we started to dance. The rhythm of the music was fast and upbeat so I tried to match my movements. All that got me was my drink sloshing over the rim of the cup and splattering on my boots.

Dom laughed and took the cup out of my hand. He walked over to a nearby booth and set down both our drinks. He gave some guy who was sitting there a fist bump and then returned to my side.

I felt the back of my neck tingling and I knew someone was watching me. I wondered if it was Dee or Blue.

Part of me hoped it was Blue, the douche. I hoped he was grinding together those pearly whites and kicking himself. 'Course, I knew he was probably making out with the girl that was practically in his lap.

Disgusted, I turned my attention back to Dom. He had somehow gotten a lot closer than before. Since we were no longer holding drinks, he had free hands… and he used them to palm my hips and pull me against him.

His hips began to move suggestively, and I stiffened slightly. Dancing was one thing. Dry-humping on the dance floor was another.

I placed my hands on his chest and pushed back.

He didn't let go.

His grip tightened.

I looked up at him. He was watching me with heavy-lidded eyes. He yanked me closer and I stumbled a bit, falling into his chest. His arms were like iron vises that went around my body, making me a prisoner in his hold.

"I can't dance this close," I yelled, hoping he would get the hint.

"We don't have to dance." His voice was so close that it raised goose bumps along my neck. It wasn't the good kind either. This guy was seriously creeping me out.

"I need some air," I said, pushing away from him again, struggling to get out of his hold.

He refused to relent. "I got all the air you need, baby."

Ew.

He did not just say that.

"Let go," I said, putting some steel behind my voice and taking a step back.

A challenging glint came into his eyes. Something inside me whispered that I just did something very wrong. I shouldn't have come here.

He started to step backward, away from the dance floor. I dug my feet into the ground, trying to stop him. It was a futile attempt because he outweighed me by a good fifty pounds.

One minute I was being dragged off the dance floor toward some dark and creepy corner, and the next I was being yanked backward, out of my captor's arms, and being deposited solidly on two shaking legs.

I noted the look of surprise on Dom's face, but it wasn't there very long.

Because someone's fist knocked it off.

I winced and looked at the guy who stepped around me, shielding me with his body. I knew that body. Blue.

He didn't stop at one punch. He leapt forward, grabbing Dom by the front of his tank and slamming his fist into his jaw again. Dom stumbled backward and then scrambled to his feet. A crowd quickly formed around us and pressed in, creating an empty circle—a ring—for the fight to continue.

I glanced around. Where the hell were the bouncers? Where was the help?

I couldn't see anything past the crush of bodies blocking us in. Help wasn't coming.

I heard another sickening thud of flesh against flesh and I whipped my gaze back to the men, where Blue was once again hammering Dom in the face.

His lip split and blood starting oozing down his chin.

Blue yanked him back once more and drew back a formidable-looking fist, but he didn't get to deliver the blow. Two guys from the crowd pounced on him, pinning him back.

"What the hell, man?" Dom said, wiping at the blood on his lip. He didn't seem surprised he was getting his ass kicked. In fact, fighting and bleeding seemed like a regular occurrence for him.

"You need to watch where you put your hands," Blue growled.

"Shit, Gray," Dom spat. "This your woman?"

Who was Gray?

"Yeah," Blue spat. "And I don't like to share." He struggled against the men holding him.

"If she's yours, what was she doing at the bar all alone? And didn't I see you with one of the crew over there in the booth?"

I saw the shift in Blue so slightly that I doubt anyone else even noticed. It was a slight tense of his shoulder muscles, as if they bunched up beneath their skin. It was like he was caught in a lie and wasn't sure what to say.

"I said *I* don't like to share. Doesn't mean I can't do what the hell I want," he said coldly.

Dom looked past Blue to me. "Damn, baby. You let him play around like that right in front of you?" he said. "Dom here wouldn't do you like that. Dom would do you right."

A growl ripped out of Blue's throat and the men pinning him back were suddenly gone. He lunged forward and tackled Dom, slamming his fist in his face once more.

There was some muffled shouting as the guys rushed Blue again, pulled him up, and pinned his arms behind his back. Dom surged to his feet and came forward, shoving a fist into Blue's gut.

Blue doubled over as Dom hit him again, this time in the face.

I screamed and rushed forward. "Stop!"

Blue might be a liar and an ass, but I couldn't watch him get beat up.

Dom glanced at me and snarled. "Shit, woman. You're a head case. Taking up for a man who will hook up right in front of you."

I swallowed. I wasn't sure what to say because he was partly right.

Blue recovered and the hands that held him let go. He straightened. "I wasn't hooking up. She's off limits to you and your crew."

Dom stepped closer and my stomach bunched. "This is my turf. Just because you used to roll down the road doesn't mean you get a free pass here."

"I never asked for a pass. I'm just here chilling like everyone else."

The crowd started to move away; clearly they thought the fight was over. I still wasn't so sure. I remained watchful and leery of both men.

"We should talk," Dom finally said after a long appraisal of Blue.

Blue shrugged like he could care less. "Sure. I'm going to see her out first." He slung an arm over my shoulders and pulled me into his side.

Damn if I didn't feel like I fit.

"C'mon. You're going home."

I thought about arguing, but I had no clue what was going on. I was buzzed, I was tired, and I was a little scared. Home sounded pretty damn awesome right then.

We moved away from the booths, walking around the dance floor. Blue didn't say anything, but kept me tightly clasped at his side. When I glanced up at him, his jaw was set and he didn't look too happy to see me. I imagined he wasn't. Getting caught being a sleazebag probably sucked.

"Where are you parked?" he asked as we neared the door.

"I didn't drive. I came here with friends."

He swore and finally looked down at me. His eyes were like swirling deep pools of blue that threatened to swallow me whole. "What the hell are you doing here tonight?"

I didn't like the tone of his voice. "Drinking away the memory of being stood up," I snapped.

The hard glint in his eyes slipped a bit.

"What's your real name?" I asked him.

His jaw clenched and he looked around to see if anyone was listening. What in the hell was going on? What was all that about?

He must have seen the questions bubbling up inside me. He reached out and wrapped a forefinger and thumb around my wrist and gave it a gentle squeeze. "You need to go home."

"I need some answers."

"What I'm doing here isn't your business."

Ouch. He was giving me a serious case of whiplash. One minute he was charming and getting me to agree to another date. The next he was standing me up, hooking up in a club, and acting like I was the last person on Earth he wanted to see.

If that wasn't enough to give me a concussion, he goes and beats up a guy who was dancing with me. Okay, fine. He was doing more than dancing. He had a serious case of grab hands. But why would Blue care? I would think he would be glad to be rid of me.

I glanced between where he held my wrist and his face.

He was bleeding.

I sighed.

"You need some ice for that eye." I started to reach up and he jerked away.

I dropped my hand like I'd been burned. I felt something embarrassing coming on… the hot rush of tears behind my eyes.

Oh hell no you don't, I told myself. *You will not cry over him.*

Dee picked the perfect time to come rushing up with Craig close behind. "Where the hell have you been?" Dee shouted.

I spun around. "I think we got separated in the crowd."

"You okay?" Dee asked, peering at me like she had X-ray vision.

"Of course, but I had too much to drink. I'm ready to go home."

When she agreed without trying to argue, I knew I must look bad. "This place sucks anyway," she said and rolled her eyes.

I smiled, but she wasn't looking at me. Her eyes had gone past me to Blue. She looked back at me and lifted her eyebrow. I rolled my eyes and hooked my arm through hers. "He's just some guy I danced with." My eyes connected with his. "I don't even know his name."

Something passed behind his eyes, something that was there and gone in the flash of a single second.

I thought he might say something; his mouth moved like he might. My heart leapt a little at the thought of an apology coming out. Yes, his apology would be dumb and too late, but I still wanted to hear it. He must have decided against it, as his lips smashed into a fine, straight line and he said nothing at all.

My heart cracked a little and I brushed past him, with Dee at my side and Craig leading the way. He followed behind us, stepping out into the parking lot, watching as we walked away.

I didn't look back. I wanted to, but I wasn't about to give him the satisfaction.

8

Blue

I stood in the shadows beside the club and watched as the black Hummer pulled out of the lot. The muscles in my back loosened, but the muscles in my chest seemed to seize.

God, I was acting like a damn woman.

I wanted to run after the car, beat on the window, and tell her how freaking sorry I was, how nothing was the way it seemed. I wanted to kiss away the moisture I saw gather behind her eyes.

I hurt her tonight.

And that pissed me off.

It pissed me off almost more than watching that asshole Dom put his hands on her. I thought I was going to pop a vein in my head when I saw her struggling as he towed her off the dance floor.

My hands clenched at my sides. What the hell was she even doing here tonight? This was the last place I would ever expect a girl like her to be.

Drinking away the memory of being stood up. Her words haunted me. A vile curse fell out of my mouth, and I stared off at the empty road.

Not only had I stood her up, but I was the reason she was in this hellhole being hit on by one of Jacksonville's biggest drug dealers. My skin crawled at the thought of what he would have done to her when they were alone.

I was glad she was gone. I wanted her safe, and being around me would clearly not be safe.

But part of me missed her. Missed what might have been.

I missed the stormy color of her eyes. I missed the way her hair fell over her forehead. I missed her smile. I wanted to know what it would be like to suck her lip into my mouth and nip at it with my teeth. I wanted to hear her moan my name in the middle of the night…

Yep. I was acting like a damn woman. A damn, horny woman.

I shoved away from the wall and walked back into the club. I wasn't sure how much damage I had done to my cover in the last few minutes, but I needed to find out.

Hell, part of me hoped my cover was blown, that I totally ruined all chances of being trusted, being pulled into whatever operation they had going on. It was impossible to have a life when you couldn't be yourself.

But this case was bigger than me. It was bigger than my life.

It sucked to have to give up something that I really wanted, but I didn't have a choice. This was my job. The safety of others was important to me. I thought about the kids that lost their life due to drugs… I thought about *everyone* who lost their life to drugs. Senseless deaths. All of them.

Cracking this case would mean helping to lower the number of senseless deaths. I wasn't naive enough to think I would stop all drug-related deaths, that I would wipe drugs off the streets for good. But I could help. I could do something. Wasn't something better than nothing?

Wasn't one life better than none?

Of course me doing my job did have its price. The price was just personal. It was costing me Julie. Yeah, we only had one date. Yeah, maybe we would go out three more times and she would hate my guts. Maybe she was the kind of girl who would nag me to death about everything and wear ugly ass granny panties beneath her sexy little clothes.

I guess I would never know.

And *that* is what sucked the most.

My option for finding out what was between us was gone.

Slater was sitting at the booth, which was surprisingly vacant… He barely looked up when I slid across the cheap vinyl seat. I picked up a beer, not knowing whose it was, and took a long pull. Then I took another.

If I hadn't known beforehand that Slater was undercover, I never would've guessed he was a cop. He had closely cropped dark hair, dark eyes, and a square jaw. A brooding and arrogant air surrounded him at all times. He fit in well with this crowd. He looked like he belonged on the streets with them. Slater barely spoke and gave the impression he barely paid attention to anything but beer and women, but I knew better.

He hid a sharp and cunning mind beneath his streetwise exterior.

I drained the rest of the beer and set it down on the table, slouching back against the booth. Slater glanced at me.

"What the hell was that?" he said.

I did a quick scan of the area around us to make sure none of the crew was listening.

"They're in the bathroom, cleaning up Dom's face."

I smirked. He was a pansy ass. I still wasn't sure how he became the quote-unquote "leader" of the organization here, but somehow he pulled it off.

"I can't believe you went at him like that," Slater said, picking up a beer and taking a sip to cover the fact he actually spoke a long sentence.

"She's off limits," I said, no room for debate in my words.

Slater studied me. "Gets messy when you work on your own turf."

I didn't say anything. But he was right. Working undercover in the same town I lived in posed a whole new set of challenges to go with the others I already faced.

"That display of temper actually bought you some points," Slater said around another large gulp of beer.

I tipped my chin as I spoke. "How?"

"You went right after the boss. No fear. Most guys—especially new ones—try to prove themselves."

"I ain't got nothing to prove."

Slater's lip curled up on the side. "Not now you don't. Word of advice?"

I spread my palms wide, inviting the advice.

"Don't do it again. He's the kind who wants strong people around him, but if he thinks you're going to try and take over, you're out."

I let those words sink in. A couple of the crew members came back to the table, giving me apprising stares. I kept my body relaxed, but inside, adrenaline pumped through me, putting me on high alert.

One of these lackey's might decide they wanted to "prove" to the boss that they got his back by coming after me.

The ring in my lower lip stung and irritated me. I didn't know how people with fifty piercings did it. I suppressed a sigh. This was just one more thing to suck up for the job.

Dom came out of the crowd and stopped to talk to a few people at a nearby booth. He picked up one of the beers and saluted the table, then turned his eyes toward me.

He sauntered over, his lip looking nice and swollen. He was going to have a black eye too. Good. He deserved that and more.

He slid into the booth next to Slater, who barely even glanced at him, and slung his elbows on the table.

"Give me one reason I shouldn't beat you down for what you pulled."

I tried to look bored. "Last time I checked, I wasn't on your payroll."

"You're at my table."

"I'll stay out of your way. You stay out of mine," I said and slid out of the booth to stand.

"Sit down," Dom ordered.

I suppressed a smile. He was a predictable tool. As much as I hated it, having Julie here tonight had actually helped me.

I glanced his way but didn't sit down.

"Why are you here?" he asked.

I gestured to the room around us. "This is a club. I came to party. Saw my man Slater"—I motioned to him and he grunted—"and decided to come say hello. I see I've worn out my welcome."

I glanced at Slater. "Later, man."

He drank some beer.

"You used to roll in Myrtle Beach?"

"Yep."

"You knew Pike?"

"Yep."

"You part of Pike's crew?"

"Nope."

Dom's eyes narrowed. My one-word responses weren't really to his liking. I had to admit, I liked pissing him off. "No?"

I half shrugged. "I was. Now I'm not."

"I told ya," Slater said to Dom. "Gray moved."

Dom narrowed his eyes suspiciously at me. I felt the muscles in my neck bunch. This is where I had to pass the test. "You were part of Pike's crew. He runs more towns than anyone I know. Why would you walk away from that much power?"

"Power wasn't mine. It's his."

"So you want your own power? Your own turf?"

"Power is too much work," I said arrogantly.

He stared at me, weighing my words. I let him look, refusing to buckle against his doubt. I knew he didn't believe me. Hell, who would? Who wouldn't want power? Power was worth almost more than money in a world like this.

Slater cleared his throat. "Gray had other things to focus on."

Dom turned his gaze away from me toward Slater, and I finally took a breath. Slater grinned a cocky grin. "Some men are more apt to be led around by their dumb handles."

Dom threw back his head and laughed. He glanced at me. "That bitch really worth all that?"

My gut tightened and anger rose up inside me at the mention of Julie. I didn't want her brought into this. Not at all. I glanced at Slater. I wanted to punch him in the face. He gave me a look, a split second of warning in his eye.

About fifty cuss words floated through my head. If I didn't say the reason I moved here was because of Julie, I was screwed.

"What can I say? I like her eyes."

Dom laughed. "Yeah, I just bet it was her eyes that had you following her up here."

I grinned suggestively.

Dom gestured to the booth so I slid in. "Man like you must be pretty bored around this Podunk town when you're used to so much action."

"I wouldn't turn down a little work."

"Lucky for you, I have an opening."

Slater stiffened slightly and reached for his beer. After he took a sip, he grabbed the blonde who was sitting beside him and started making out.

"An opening?" I asked, looking away from Slater and not so much as glancing back.

"One of my crew had to take a leave of absence."

"Why?" Slater was still kissing the blonde, but I knew damn well he was listening.

"He got a little too ambitious."

I wasn't sure what that meant, but I knew not to press the issue even though I really wanted to. Instead of asking straight out, I said, "So what happens when he comes back and I took his job?"

"He ain't coming back."

That didn't sound very good. I forced myself to smile slowly. "Well, it looks like it's my lucky day."

"I'll be in touch," he said and then slid out of the booth and turned to walk away. Then he glanced back. "One thing," he said.

I flicked my gaze up to his.

"You ever touch me again, I'll kill you."

I felt Slater's adrenaline rush, his sudden hawk-like attention. I didn't dare look his way. I thought it would be a dead giveaway something was up. I stayed lounged in my seat. His threat didn't scare me. I realized maybe it should, but I couldn't bring myself to care.

I think my lack of reaction got under his skin because he added, "And don't keep that little piece hidden. She'd look good at my table."

My teeth ground together. I wanted to plow my fist into his face so bad that my insides quaked with it. *Stay cool,* I reminded myself. If I showed Julie was any kind of weakness for me, it could be dangerous for her.

Luckily, he didn't seem to want a response because he finally left. Thank God too, because the more I looked at him, the more I wanted to beat his ass.

Most everyone at the table followed him. I watched as he slid into another of "his" booths and then I looked away.

A waitress came by with a tray full of drinks. I grabbed one. "Hey!" she said, annoyed.

I pulled a couple bills out of my pants and slid them in the front pocket of her apron. "Thanks, sweet cheeks."

The annoyance slipped right off her face and she winked.

I downed the drink, knowing I shouldn't drink any more, but not caring. This night had been all kinds of messed up.

Slater and I sat there a while, bullshitting with the girls, listening to the music and Slater making out with any girl he could get his hands on. Man, he really got into his undercover role.

After a while, I slid out of the booth. "Later, man."

He pulled away from the brunette in his lap and got out of the booth to offer me his fist. I bumped mine against his and he said, "He's gonna check you out with Pike. You pass that and you're in."

I'd pass. I knew I would.

Slater clapped me on the shoulder and leaned in. "Thanks for the info."

I didn't acknowledge his words as I walked away. Is that why he was undercover? Was he investigating the "leave of absence" by one of the crew? I thought he was called in for the drugs as well, but now I was beginning to wonder if maybe there was more.

9

Julie

I pretended to be drunker than I was on the ride home. I didn't want to face Dee's never-ending questions about the guy she saw me with, the other guy I was dancing with, and if I saw what happened when a fight broke out.

Luckily, she had been too far away to see I was practically in the center of the fight. Luckily, she didn't know what Blue looked like, because if she'd realized the man in the gray knit cap was Blue, there might have been a second fight that night.

I leaned my head against the cool glass of the backseat window and stared out into the darkness. Every once in a while, I would let my eyes droop closed so Dee would think I was close to passing out. Really, I wasn't nearly drunk enough.

The alcohol I did drink seemed to vacate my system the minute Blue started beating up the guy I was dancing with. My eyes closed again, this time not because I was trying to fool Dee, but because I couldn't stop thinking about him.

The way it felt to be pressed into his side as he steered me toward the exit. It was a casual touch, but I was close enough that I felt the tension in his muscles; I felt the awareness in his body. It didn't make me afraid… It made me feel protected.

I wasn't the kind of girl who needed to be protected. I lived alone, I took care of myself, and I refused to rely on a man. But that didn't mean the inner princess in me didn't squeal in delight when his arm draped around me and I felt small.

Even tough girls want to feel safe sometimes, too.

When Craig pulled the Hummer up to my house, I got out quickly, shocking them with my movements. Dee probably thought she was going to have to peel me off the backseat to get me inside.

She climbed out of the SUV and met me on the sidewalk. I smiled at her. "Thanks for the ride and for the fun."

"You gonna be okay?" she asked, concerned.

My heart softened at her genuine concern, and I pulled her into a big hug. Maybe the alcohol was still in there somewhere after all. "Thanks, Dee. You're the best."

"I know," she agreed when I pulled away. "I'll walk you in."

"You don't have to," I said, grabbing my keys. "I'll be fine. I'm going to pass out anyway."

"Call me tomorrow."

"You know it."

I knew she wouldn't leave until I was inside, so I trudged up the steps and unlocked the front door. It took a couple tries to get the door open because my hands were shaking and my vision was slightly blurry. Yeah, the alcohol was definitely still there.

Still, I couldn't pretend.

I couldn't pretend that everything I was feeling was liquor-induced. The blurred vision, yeah. The exhaustion I was feeling? Probably the liquor. But the shaking? That was all Blue.

Once I was inside, I waved to her and Craig and then shut the door and leaned against it. The quiet serenity of my home enveloped me like a giant hug. I sighed in relief. I was so on my way to becoming one of those crazy old women who lived alone and watched reruns of Jeopardy all day long.

Upstairs, I yanked off my boots and clothes, leaving them in a giant heap in the center of the floor. I padded into the bathroom to wash off my makeup and comb out my hair. I clipped my bangs away from my face with a little pink clip that was lying on the edge of the sink.

After pulling on a too-big T-shirt, I crawled into bed and sighed.

I closed my eyes.

I saw his face.

My eyes sprang back open.

I sat up, yanked the clip out of my hair, and tossed it across the room, where I heard it clatter in the darkness. A frustrated growl vibrated my throat as I kicked the blankets around frantically, freeing my feet and twisting the sheets into a pile in the center of the mattress.

My stomach seemed to revolt from all the movement and my head began to pound.

"Really?" I yelled in the darkness. "I'm going to get a nasty hangover from one and a half drinks?"

I leaned back against my padded headboard and tried to calm my rolling stomach. As I sat there, trying not to barf, a light sound caught my attention.

It was the closing of the front door.

I perked up, forgetting all about the fact I was suffering from an attack of an unsuspecting hangover.

Had I forgotten to lock the door? I never *forgot* to lock the door. But I was usually not running from my best friend.

Great.

The one time I don't lock the damn door is the one time a burglar decides to come a' calling.

Too bad for mister criminal I had a plan for something like this. I was the kind of girl that *always* had a plan.

I crept into the bathroom, being as quiet as I could, and reached into the cabinet. I pulled out my weapons (hey, all the crap women have to do to themselves to look good definitely qualify as weapons) and gripped them closely to my chest with both hands.

My heart was beating so hard against my ribs that it actually hurt and I had to work to not gasp for breath. Catching my intruder by surprise was key to my plan.

Moving quickly through the dark, I moved to the bedroom door, leaning against the wall and peering out into the darkened hallway. I could see the top of the stairs from where I stood, as well as the railing that ran alongside the hallway to keep someone from falling into the stairwell from upstairs.

Courtesy of the nightlight down in the entryway (it came in handy when I wanted a drink in the middle of the night); I saw a shadow move against the wall. The figure was large and distorted against the tall bare wall of the stairwell.

Up until that point, I hadn't been certain someone was in the house.

But now I couldn't deny it.

There was a robber in my house.

He for sure had nefarious plans.

Too bad for him I had a really shitty night and wasn't in the mood.

As his foot stepped on the bottom stairs, I slinked out the door and along the wall, keeping my eyes trained on the top of the stairs. He began climbing (I was very unimpressed with his quietness, or rather lack thereof), and as he climbed, I slipped along the wall, moving through the darkness until I was standing in the corner directly across from the top of the stairs.

I saw his shoulders appear as he continued upward. He was wearing a dark coat and a dark hat… He was nothing but a large, ominous shape in the night.

I swallowed. The sound of my saliva scraping down my dry throat made me wince, and my palms were sweaty, causing me to tighten my grip on my weapons.

Oh yeah. I forgot.

I had weapons. I had a plan.

Just as his foot cleared the top step, I gave a battle cry and leapt forward, brandishing my weapon—a very large can of hairspray—which I pointed and pressed down on the top.

The can hissed as a cloud of very nice-smelling spray rushed out into the space between us. The man yelled, caught off guard, and slapped a hand over his eyes. I sprayed him some more as he stumbled forward.

I rushed past him, still holding on to the hairspray, going for the stairs. I was NOT the kind of idiot girl in the movies who ran farther into the house. I was headed for the freaking front door.

The man, now sputtering, turned and grabbed the hem of my shirt and pulled me backward. I stumbled forward and would have fallen right down the stairs, but he yanked me away.

My hands flew out to protect myself from falling and the can of hairspray rolled down the steps.

"Shit," I grunted and I rolled onto my back, twisting away from his grasp. He released me but then reached down for me again.

I screamed and struck out with my last remaining weapon. A pink razor. Hey, if it could tame the hair on my legs, then it could take out an attacker.

I pushed the blade down on his hand and pulled back the handle.

"Fuck!" he yelled, jerking away.

I fell back on the carpet, breathing hard. He was hunched over his poor razored hand, and I drew my foot back to kick him.

"Shit, Julie. It's me!"

My foot paused in midair.

The hall light flipped on.

Blue stood over me with a look of pained frustration on his face. I lay there stunned. He was the last freaking person I expected to see. In fact, if asked to guess who would be more likely to be in my home in the middle of the night, Blue or a burglar, I would not have chosen Blue.

Maybe I was a lot drunker than I thought.

"Blue?" I asked tentatively.

His gaze dropped a little lower than my face, and I realized I still had my foot raised in the air… and I wasn't wearing pants.

Well, shit.

I jumped to my feet quickly, letting the oversized shirt fall to my knees.

"Is that a razor?" he asked, blinking at the handle clutched in my hand.

I nodded dumbly.

He lifted his hand, which was bleeding freely, and looked at it, then back at me. "You gouged my hand with a pink razor," he said, almost like he was talking to himself.

Then he blinked his eyes and wiped at his face. "Did you spray me with hairspray?"

"What did you expect?" I said irritably. "You broke into my house."

He sighed dramatically. "I needed to see you."

Okay, those five little words completely made my stomach turn over. Butterflies erupted and caused my insides to tremble.

Those feelings coupled with the adrenaline, the alcohol, and the fear were not a good combination.

I slapped a hand over my mouth and rushed back through my room and into the bathroom, where I fell to my knees in front of the toilet and proceeded to hurl.

Gah, throwing up was like the grossest thing ever. And the sounds my body made… It was like a tiny alien was crawling its way out of my body and torturing me in the process.

My back heaved and pain sliced through my sides. My body was so desperate to get rid of everything that was bothering it that my heaves were violent.

I felt someone crouch behind me and sweep my hair off my face. The cool air that brushed over my neck felt blissful.

"It's okay," Blue whispered rubbing his palm in slow circles across my back. My body relaxed beneath his touch. I would have been angry at my body's response if I wasn't feeling so lousy.

After my stomach emptied its entire contents and a cold sweat had broken out over my skin, I finally stopped heaving. My body was utterly exhausted and I just wanted to collapse. I sat back away from the toilet and my body slid toward the floor.

Blue was there and he lifted me up into his arms and carried me gently into the bedroom and walked toward the bed.

"What the hell happened to your bed?" he asked, eyeballing the heap of covers in the center.

"I was asleep when you broke in," I muttered.

He shoved the blankets aside and laid me down. "How much did you drink tonight?" he asked, gently pushing a damp strand of hair off my cheek.

I groaned. "One rum and coke and a shot of vodka."

"That's it?" he asked skeptically.

"And a couple sips of another rum and coke."

He was silent for a long time, and I cracked my eyes open and looked at him. Even with only the light from the bathroom, I could see he was frowning and pale.

"What?"

"Jules," he began, sitting down beside me, causing my body to slide closer to him as the mattress dipped.

He called me Jules.

I liked it.

"Hey," he said, calling me back from my swooning. "Did he give you anything to drink… anything at all?"

I knew who the "he" was that Blue was talking about. "You mean like drugs?"

He nodded stiffly.

"No. I would never take drugs."

"Did he buy you a drink?"

I knew he was thinking of the date rape drug.

"No. He didn't. I wouldn't have drunk it anyway."

My words didn't seem to make him feel better. He gazed down at me with worry lacing his face. I sighed. "I never drink, okay? I didn't eat dinner so that just made it worse."

He ran a hand over his head, pulling off the knit cap as he went and tossing it on the floor. Then he stood and paced to the end of the bed. "This is all my fault," he muttered.

You know… I had imagined a time when Blue was here in my bedroom with me and this was not the scene I was picturing.

Disappointment crackled over me and I sat up, swinging my legs over the bed.

"I think you should lie down," Blue said, coming over to my side.

"I think you should tell me what the hell a cop is doing breaking and entering." I glanced at him with narrowed eyes. "You are a cop, aren't you?"

He barked a laugh. "Yes."

I stared at him, waiting for the explanation I deserved.

"Your front door was unlocked," he said sternly. Like it was somehow *my* fault he invited himself in.

"I have a doorbell."

"I don't want anyone to know I'm here."

I sighed. "What the hell is going on, Blue?"

He fell silent again and resumed pacing, like he wasn't sure what he wanted to say. I pushed up off the bed and headed into the bathroom. "I'm going to clean up," I told him before shutting the door and locking it.

I had no idea if a lock would keep him out, but I did it anyway.

I grabbed a can of Lysol from under the sink and sprayed it around the toilet, closing the lid. Then I stripped off my shirt and threw it in the hamper sitting inside the closet. After grabbing the pink razor off the floor where I dropped it and tossing it in the trash, I took a quick shower.

The cool water felt wonderful against my sticky skin. As I washed, I rinsed out my mouth. I still felt lightly queasy and a little weak, but I knew my throwing up was over. As I dried off and combed out my hair, I wondered if Blue would still be here when I walked out.

He had a tendency of hanging around long enough to mess with my emotions and then disappearing without explanation. After I pulled on a pair of sleep shorts and a T-shirt, I glanced at myself in the mirror.

Do not get sucked in by his good looks, authoritive and sexy demeanor. He will tie you up in a knot that you have no hope of untying.

I glanced at the toilet where the finest hours of my evening were spent (uh, not).

He will also make you tipsy.

Once my self-imposed lecture was over, I pushed away from the sink and opened the door. I half expected the room to be empty.

It wasn't what I expected.

The bed was remade, the covers all smoothed out perfectly. The small lamp beside the bed provided a bit of illumination, and he was sitting on the floor with his back to the wall.

I flipped off the bathroom light and stepped into the bedroom, my stomach doing that funny flip-flopping thing again.

"Feel better?" he asked, his voice low.

"Yeah."

He pushed up and grabbed a bottle of water off the nightstand, unscrewed the cap, and held it out.

"Thank you," I said, taking a dainty sip.

He picked up a bottle of pain reliever and shook out two in his very large palm, which he extended to me.

I plucked them out of his hand. "Looks like you found your way around my kitchen."

"Figured you could use this."

I swallowed the pills and noticed the paper towels wrapped around the hand that I gouged with my razor. I also noted the gash on his cheekbone from the hit he took earlier at the club. He was in no better shape than I was.

I retreated into the bathroom, grabbed a first aid kit, and dampened a fresh cloth with cool water. "Sit," I instructed when I had all my supplies.

He glanced at the only place in the room to sit. The bed.

I sighed. "Go on."

He turned and walked toward the end of the bed. I couldn't help but admire the way his butt looked in his jeans. I was totally a butt girl.

Once he was sitting on the end of the bed, I laid out the first aid supplies and then brought the cloth up to his face to wipe away the dried blood. He didn't say a word. He just watched me intently with that wide indigo stare; his eyes never left my face.

It was a little unnerving.

"This might hurt," I said quietly because the silence was just too loud.

He didn't even flinch as I cleaned his skin, lightly stroking over his very smooth cheekbone.

"Does it hurt?"

"No."

I noticed his skin felt slightly stiff, and I giggled. I got him good with that hairspray. He raised his eyebrow in silent inquiry as I snickered.

"Your skin is stiff." I giggled some more.

He cracked a smile. "What the hell were you thinking?"

"That I could blind you with my hairspray, attack you with my razor, and then escape out the front door."

He rolled his eyes. "That's the best you could come up with when you thought you had an intruder?"

"Hey," I admonished. "That was not a hasty plan. That was well thought out."

"You *planned* that?" he asked incredulously.

"A girl needs to have a plan," I said sensibly, setting aside the cloth and reaching for a bit of antibacterial cream.

"Let me get this straight." He began. "You don't lock your door at night and your idea of a plan to save yourself from a home invasion is a pink razor and a can of hairspray?"

He said it like it was a bad idea.

"The door was an accident," I explained and leaned closer to dab a little of the cream on his cheek. It wasn't a bad cut. I figured it would be healed in a week or so.

I pulled back a little to study my handiwork. "I don't think it needs a bandage."

"Bandages are for girls."

I smiled, but when our gazes crashed, an odd sort of feeling came over me and it was hard to breathe. Without thinking, I reached up and traced the cleft in his chin, my forefinger dipping in gently and then sliding across his jaw.

His eyes were closed when I pulled away and he had this look… this look of peace on his face. On impulse, I brushed a lock of hair off his forehead.

Then I realized that I was doing exactly what I said I wouldn't and pulled away. "Let me see your hand," I said, ignoring the fact my voice sounded like I hadn't spoken in days.

He held it out between us and I pulled away the red-dotted paper towel. The cut was fairly deep and a little jagged. Probably because my razor had three rows of blades. A little pinch of guilt stung my chest when I realized I'd done this to him.

Then I reminded myself he didn't knock. And he stood me up.

I didn't feel as bad after that.

I dabbed at the cut with the cloth, noting that it was still bleeding lightly. I applied some more of the antibacterial cream and then pulled out a couple bandages. He made a sound, and I smiled. "Care to change your previous statement about bandages and girls?"

"How about bandages applied by girls are manly."

I snorted and worked in silence. The whole time I fixed him up, I avoided his stare and I avoided touching him more than necessary.

When he was cleaned up, I noted the redness on his knuckles. I ran my fingertips over the skin. "Is this from earlier?"

"Yeah."

I sat back on my haunches and gazed up at him.

"What the hell is going on? What are you doing here?"

His answer was the last thing I expected.

10

Blue

Her touch made me wish the guy landed more punches. Her touch made me wish the cut on my hand was just a little bit worse.

Her touch made me want to touch her. To reach out and cup her face in my palm, to stroke the side of her neck with my thumb… to press my lips completely against hers.

In that moment I wasn't an undercover cop. She wasn't pissed at me for all the shitty stuff I'd done. I was just a guy sitting in front of a girl whose heart made mine beat a little unevenly.

I knew I shouldn't be here. Involving her in any aspect of my life was just wrong.

Yet here I was. She was like my own personal siren, calling me closer, towing me in.

At first I thought I could come here, give her a lame excuse for my behavior, and make it so she wasn't so mad at me. The thought of her out there day after day, thinking bad thoughts about me was unacceptable.

I knew we couldn't be together, but I couldn't stand her hating me.

But then she attacked me.

Like a little fierce hell cat, dashing out of the dark with a can of hairspray and a freaking pink razor. I would laugh if it didn't scare me to the balls of my feet.

She definitely wasn't a damsel in distress. Anyone who crossed her would have a hell of a fight.

But in the end she wouldn't win.

She was too small, to naïve, and far too unprepared.

Any woman whose best plan was a can of hairspray needed some serious help. My skin crawled with what could have happened here tonight if I hadn't been the one to walk through her door. Shit, she was half drunk, uncoordinated, and sick as hell.

I'd never seen anyone throw up so much after so few drinks.

Of course, I wasn't a fool. I knew it hadn't just been the alcohol that sent her racing into the bathroom. It was a culmination of events, many of them (okay, all of them) entirely my fault.

How the hell did she get so wrapped up in all of this so fast?

That first haircut was a mistake on so many levels.

But every time I looked at her, I wanted to keep making the same "mistake" over and over again.

"Blue?" she asked softly, getting up from her place beside me and packing up the first aid kit.

I blinked and watched her move. "Sorry. I was just thinking."

"About what?"

"About my answer." She asked me what was going on. I should lie. I should make something up. I should be a jerk and piss her off so she would never come near me again.

I wasn't going to.

"You're not going to tell me anything are you?" she said, coming out of the bathroom and standing in the center of the room, watching me.

She looked so damn cute in her little cotton shorts and striped T-shirt. Her hair was damp and ruffled and her cheeks were pale.

"I shouldn't," I began, and her shoulders slumped. "But I am."

Her eyes snapped up to mine.

"We had a good time on our first date, right?" I began.

Her eyes narrowed and her jaw jutted out a little stubbornly. "Are you fishing for compliments?"

"No." I sighed. "It just seemed like we had a really good time."

"And then you never called." She finished.

"It wasn't because I didn't want to."

"Oh?" she asked, crossing her arms over her chest. "Let me guess. You lost your phone. No wait, your dog ate my number. Then you lost your memory and forgot where I lived."

"I don't have a dog," I quipped.

She didn't think it was funny.

I sighed. "Right after I dropped you off that night, I got called into work." She didn't shoot out a smartass comeback so I figured I had her attention. "I got assigned a case that kept me out of town for a long time."

"They didn't have phones where you went?"

"Yes, but I wasn't allowed to have contact with anyone I knew. Not even my family."

Her eyes widened. "Like you went undercover?"

"Yes."

"Where?"

"I'd really rather not say."

Her lips pursed. I sighed. "It's for your safety."

She seemed to accept that, thankfully. "How long were you gone?"

"I got back two weeks before I came in for a haircut."

I watched the realization come over her features. She looked at me closely. "You were gone all those months?"

"Yes."

"That's why your hair was so long when you came into the salon that day," she said, almost like she was talking to herself.

"Yeah, and now it's all short and clean-cut looking," I muttered, wishing I hadn't cut it.

Her eyes went to the floor where I tossed the hat I was wearing. "You were covering up how short it was?"

I nodded.

"Why would it matter now?"

"Because they put me back undercover. Tonight."

"Tonight," she scoffed.

I scooted up onto the bed and leaned against the headboard. Then I patted the mattress beside me, inviting her closer. She hesitated for a second but then crawled over the top blankets and settled beside me.

"I couldn't call you. I had to turn in my phone and my car. The rules of going undercover are strict. Especially since I'm going undercover in this town."

"They took your phone and your car?"

"Yes. And I'm not to go to the station or my house, or anywhere else I might normally go for the foreseeable future."

She rolled her head to the side and stared up at me. "But you're here."

"I shouldn't be," I said softly, gazing into her face. There was something about her… something that just made it hard to stay away. Like she emitted some kind of secret gravity, the kind of gravity that pulled in only me (it better not be pulling in anyone else).

"Why are you here, Blue?"

"I couldn't stand the thought of you thinking bad about me."

"Oh, I was thinking hateful things," she said, her voice low.

I laughed. "Yeah, I know."

"So, tonight…" Her voice trailed away.

On impulse I reached over and threaded my fingers through hers resting in her lap. "Tonight I really wanted to go out with you."

A soft smile played on the corners of her mouth, but then she blinked and looked away. I took it as a good sign that she left her hand in mine. "At the club…"

"The club was a freaking cluster-fuck." I blew out a breath.

"You were undercover there?"

"Yeah, I was working on my cover."

"What's the case about?" she asked tentatively.

"Drugs."

Her eyes widened. "Is that why you asked me about drugs and my drink?"

I nodded. "That guy you were dancing with, he's a dealer. He's dangerous, Julie. Stay away from him. From that club."

She shuddered. "I have no intention of ever going near either again."

"Hey," I said softly, pulling her chin around so she could look into my face. "Did he hurt you?"

"No." Her voice was breathless and it made desire spark through my veins.

Without thought, I dropped a kiss to her forehead. She froze, like she didn't know what to do. I smiled against her skin and then dropped my forehead down to lean against hers. "I'm sorry I stood you up tonight."

"Duty calls," she replied.

"Yeah. Sometimes I really hate my job."

"How long are you going to be undercover?"

I released her chin and leaned my head back against the headboard. "I don't know. 'Til the case is over."

"This is the same case you were on before?"

I nodded. "It's the same case. Different location. It turns out things are happening closer to home than we realized."

"Those things are drugs?"

"Yeah. Dealing has become a big problem farther south, and apparently the supplier lives here."

"Wow," she intoned, leaning her head against the headboard. Then she jerked suddenly, like there was a sudden explosion of sound. Except the only sound was that of our breathing. My body tensed instinctively and my eyes scanned the room.

"What's wrong?" I swear just being near her kicked my testosterone into high gear and had me thinking all these caveman thoughts. *Mine. Protect. Claim.*

"Is this dangerous?" she asked, her stormy eyes wide.

I shrugged. It was dangerous. Drug dealers were no joke. They were territorial, they were mean, and they only thought about the job. But the look on her face had me keeping my mouth shut. Clearly this idea scared her. She was likely wondering what kind of danger she was in now.

Julie yanked her fingers out of mine and wrapped her hand around my wrist, squeezing a little. "Could you get hurt?"

I paused. "What?"

"Blue," she said, exasperated, giving my arm a jerk. "Could you get hurt?"

"You're worried about me?" I asked, astonishment flowing through me like a river in a rainstorm. I hadn't expected such stark concern on her face. I hadn't expected her to completely bowl me over.

"Well, yeah," she said, like it was a no-brainer.

I couldn't take it.

Not another single second.

I slipped my hands along her ribcage and lifted her off the mattress, depositing her on my lap. Her bare legs straddled my thighs as I settled her a little bit closer. Slowly, I drew my fingers down the sides of her ribs so I could grip that soft spot around her waist, just above her hip bones.

Julie stared at me curiously, her hands falling between us. It took a minute of convincing, but I got my hands to leave her waist and cupped her face, brushing my thumbs along the creamy satin of her cheeks.

I pulled her in, keeping my eyes locked on hers, feeling the slight trembling of my insides. I never anticipated anyone or anything so much. I never before wanted to prolong the torture of waiting for the first touch of a woman's lips on mine.

Her eyes fluttered closed and the softest sigh escaped her slightly parted lips.

I crushed our mouths together, mingling our breath, taking claim on exactly what I wanted. Her lips were moist and soft. Her kiss was giving, like she was offering up every single piece of herself, like she was laying herself bare and trusting me to keep her safe.

Holy hell, I would die to kiss her like this every day for the rest of my life.

I held her face still, being greedy with my need. My lips ravaged her mouth, being gentle but leaving behind nothing. I nipped at the corner of her lips and rang my tongue around the edges. My bottom lip fit so perfectly in the center of hers that they joined together like two halves of a whole.

When I wanted more, I pressed my thumbs into her jaw, ever so lightly, and her lips parted so I could sweep my tongue into her luscious mouth.

She tasted like toothpaste, like cool mint. It was a stark contrast against the heat of the kiss, the heat that was pulsing between us.

Her hands found the front of my shirt and she gripped it, taking large fistfuls and pulling herself closer to me. Her tongue swept the roof of my mouth, and I groaned, my pulse picking up as all the blood in my body rushed to the area between my legs.

With a deep groan, I ripped my mouth away from hers and she grabbed me back, covering my lips with hers, gently coercing my piercing into her mouth to roll it around her tongue. The gentle tugging sensation was unlike anything I felt before. Need slammed into my body. All the blood left my head and traveled south. All the air left my lungs, and the only thought I could summon was telling me to take her then and there.

She made a little purring sound and released the piercing, pressing a full kiss against my lips before she collapsed forward, burying her face in my neck. Every so often her lips would brush against my beating pulse and desire would sweep me all over again.

I put a leash around my lust and told it to heal. This wasn't what I came here for.

No. That was a lie.

This is *exactly* what I came here for. She was exactly what I wanted.

It was bad timing. The worst.

How the hell was I going to do my job *and* keep Julie in my life?

11

Julie

Whoa.

It wasn't much of a word, but it was a hell of a feeling.

I didn't just bury my face in his neck because I couldn't get close enough (can you blame me?). I did it because I needed a minute to compose myself. I felt like a pair of well-worn jeans, comfortable and stretched to the perfect fit. His lap was exactly right. It was almost a shame, really. Because now no other seat would fit me like this. I would always be wanting the feeling of being against him.

But like a well-worn pair of jeans, I had a hole in my pocket and stuff was falling out. Like my emotions. Like my heart. If I looked at him right now, he would see it. He would know.

I'd never kissed anyone with a piercing in their lip before. That little silver ring begged to be sucked on, and I couldn't resist tugging it into my mouth. The metal was cool against my fevered body.

And his lips… bloody hell.

It almost made me mad all over again that he hadn't kissed me on our first date. He withheld such a blissful moment from me for far too long.

I thought it was because he wasn't interested. I thought it was because my feelings were one-sided.

My feelings were so not one-sided.

There was no way in hell he could kiss me like that if he wasn't into me.

A little giggle escaped my lips and I cut it off, hoping he didn't hear my epic display of girly giddiness.

His broad, heavy palm slid up my back. "What's so funny?"

I pressed my nose against his neck and smiled. "Nothing."

"Are you seriously still drunk?" he asked, a hint of speculation in his tone.

After all the hurling I had done? Not likely. "I'm just tipsy." *On you.*

I'd like to retract my previous statement that people could not get tipsy on other people. They totally could.

I snuggled a little bit closer, tucking my hands between us, feeling the steady rhythm of his heart against the backs of my palms. When both his arms wrapped around me, I was totally surrounded by him.

It was a feeling I'd never experienced before.

It was all-encompassing. It was all-powerful. It was all I ever wanted.

I felt safe. I felt warm. I was so utterly comfortable against him that I couldn't imagine being anywhere else. I didn't think about his track record of disappointing me. Or that after tonight I probably wouldn't see him again.

For several long, blissful moments, I just existed in his arms and everything else melted away.

Reality creeped in slowly. I knew that there were likely a hundred questions that I should be asking… but honestly, I couldn't think of one. It wasn't because I didn't care or that Blue being undercover didn't interest me. Everything about Blue interested me. I wasn't big on reading, but if he was a book, I would read him cover to cover. Over and over again.

It's just that… none of that stuff mattered. Not really. It was quite clear to me that I was vulnerable to him. It seemed it didn't matter what he did to me; I still wanted him.

But my wanting him didn't change that he wasn't available.

With a sigh, I pushed up off his chest, and his arms slid down to loop loosely around my hips. I couldn't bring myself to pull completely away so I left my hands resting on his chest.

"So you're an undercover cop," I said, my eyes taking in all of his features and his mussed up hair.

"Yep."

"You don't know how long this case will last?"

"No."

"And if I see you out, I should pretend I don't know you?"

He frowned. "You're not going to see me."

"Just like I wasn't supposed to see you tonight?" I countered.

He gave me a look. The kind of look that said "are you seriously challenging me right now?" I guess maybe I was. I yanked my hands away from his chest and crossed my arms to stare at him. I was waiting for my answer.

He studied me. "You aren't going to be visiting any more places like that."

"Says who?" I asked, lifting my eyebrows. Surely he wasn't trying to boss me around.

"Says me."

My gaze slipped away from his glare and down to the little ring in his lip. It was so close… I could just lean forward and—

He made a sound deep in his throat and took my face in his hands, forcing my gaze up. "Stop that."

"I've never kissed anyone with a lip piercing."

"I'm your first, huh?"

I nodded. "Is that part of your cover?"

He brushed a thumb across my bottom lip. "Yeah."

"I like it." I admitted, looking at it once again.

"Do you now?" he asked, smiling slightly.

"Does it hurt?"

"It's very painful," he said, a sly look coming into his eyes. "You should kiss it. Make it better."

I reached up and pulled his hands away from my face and leaned forward. My chest brushed against his as I tentatively drew the silver ring between my lips. My tongue swept across the skin, lavishing the area with warm moisture, and he groaned.

Feeling a little bolder I rocked forward, the area between my legs rubbing against his jeans, and tugged a little harder on the ring as I slipped my tongue through the center.

Blue gripped my hips and squeezed, holding me against him, causing this needy, throbbing sensation within the folds of my vagina.

After I kissed and played with the piercing, I untangled my tongue and pulled back, but he seized forward and caught me up in a full-on kiss. His arms locked around me and he rolled, pinning me to the mattress, the pillows at my back.

The weight of his body pinned me down as his lips ravished my mouth and his knee worked its way up between my thighs. I gripped his biceps, wrapping my hands around them and holding on, my hips squirming around looking for something I knew he could give me.

When his jean-clad knee connected right at my center, the hard pressure of him made me cry out, but the sound was swallowed with another sweeping kiss. His hand shoved between us and covered my breast. The nipple hardened and rose up to meet him, begging for more attention.

I didn't know how he kissed me so thoroughly and groped me at the same time, but it was so insanely pleasurable that all thought fled from my brain. All I could think about was more. I wanted more. And less.

More of him. Less of the clothes between us.

Blue ripped away his mouth, panting. He pushed himself up, keeping his weight off me with both his arms. "I should go."

"Yeah," I agreed.

Neither of us moved.

He stared at me for a few more moments, his eyes seeming to take in every last detail of my face before he slowly started to lower himself back down. It was almost like he was warning me that he was coming. Like I would push him off or try to get away.

I wasn't going anywhere. I wanted his lips on mine like a little kid wanted an ice cream cone.

I kept my eyes open, watching him, not wanting to miss a single thing about his expression. I enjoyed the way his pupils dilated with desire and his nostrils flared out just ever so slightly. I enjoyed the way his biceps shook on either side of my head as if keeping himself from touching me was the hardest thing he'd ever done. He stopped short, just centimeters separating our lips as he stared into my eyes.

My stomach was doing some crazy gymnastics, vaulting around inside my middle like I'd just gone on a roller coaster ride with fifty loops and curves. If my heart beat any more erratically, I might go into cardiac arrest.

And then he closed the distance. His lips brushed over mine; the contact was nothing short of jolting. It was like I hadn't just spent the last ten minutes making out with him like a horny teenager. It was as if I had never kissed him at all.

Every single thing about him washed over me. I felt like I was standing on top of a cliff, ready to dive off. Anxious, delicious desire curled tightly around me, winding me up so tight that I was afraid I might snap.

I dug my fingers into the blankets, twisting the soft fabric around my hands and gripping it tightly, hoping it would keep me grounded.

But nothing could keep me from getting lost in Blue.

It was as if I were Alice in Wonderland and he was the hole I fell through.

His lips didn't lift one time. The kiss was continuous; it went on forever. It wasn't demanding.

It wasn't the kind that made my hips gyrate beneath him. It was something that went beyond the search for an epic orgasm. It was the kind of kiss that went further than my desire. It went deeper than my vagina. Something about the way his lips lingered on mine, softly caressing me with his tongue, made the beating of my heart slow to a lazy, lethargic thump.

Thump.

Thump.

Thump.

When our lips finally stopped touching, he looked at me once more. My vision was slightly skewed. I blinked, bringing him and his amazing azure eyes back into focus.

"Come on," he said, his voice whisper soft. "I want you to lock the door behind me."

Even after he moved off the bed, I lay there and stared up at the ceiling. I wasn't sure my heart rate would ever be the same again. How in the hell was I supposed to not want him, to not be angry at his jerk-face ways when he freaking kissed me like that?

Blue did not play fair.

Even still, when he offered his hand as I pushed up off the bed, I accepted.

After putting the knit cap back onto his head, I followed him out of the bedroom and down the stairs into my darkened living room. The soft glow of the nightlight in the stairwell was the only illumination by the front door.

Blue turned to me, nothing but a shape in the dark. "Promise me you'll stay out of that bar."

"I already told you I would," I said, exasperated.

"Lay low for a while," he said. I could feel his stare. "Unfortunately you've been connected with my new identity."

"Should I call you Gray?"

"You don't have to call me anything because you won't see me again."

My stomach sank. My heart rate sped up. Disappointment was an ugly kind of feeling. "If you planned to never see me again, why did you come here at all?" I said, irritation seeping into my tone. When was he going to stop doing this to me? When was he going to stop getting under my skin, working his way into my chest… only to deny me what I truly wanted.

Damn. It was too late to take that thought back. I couldn't even convince myself of that lie. I wanted Blue; nothing was going to change that. It was very apparent that he was like my own personal brand of drug.

He heaved a great sigh and stepped forward. I stepped back. His hands dropped to his waist. "I told you. I can't stand the thought of you… hating me."

Oh, I didn't hate him. But I wanted to.

"So you thought making out with me and then taking off into the night would make me less mad?"

"This isn't forever," he whispered, stepping forward. "Eventually this case will be over."

"So?"

"So then maybe you and I…"

"Are you asking me to wait for you?"

He was silent a long moment. He sighed heavily. "Yeah, I guess I am."

"So you expect me to sit around here for God knows how long and wonder if you're making out with some random chick in a seedy bar across town? You expect me to wonder day after day if you're hurt or if your cover was blown and someone wants to kill you?"

To his credit, he didn't try to talk his way out of that one. He didn't try to deny what he did was dangerous and if he had to make out with some girl, he would. If he'd tried to deny it, I would have lost some respect for him because he would have been lying.

"I get it," he said eventually, not making another move toward me. I ached for him. I ached for that minimal distance between us to be gone. I ached for those moments spent up in my bedroom when I was in his arms. He turned and grabbed the door handle. But he didn't pull it open.

His voice was quiet, but it carried all the way to my ears.

"I wouldn't wait for me either. But, I just… I want you to know something."

"What?" my voice was hoarse.

"This isn't me choosing my job over you. I don't have a choice. Not really. I have to do this. I'm already in too deep."

Silence fell like a thick blanket over the room. Yet neither of us moved.

His words pierced my chest. My heart returned to that slow rhythm of thumping he inspired.

"If I had it to do all over again…" he said, still keeping his back to me. "That night after our first date, I wouldn't take the assignment. I would have told them no. I would have chosen you."

All the air in my lungs whooshed out of me.

"Lock this door," he said, slipping outside into the deep cover of night.

I stared at the spot he just vacated, hearing his words for the second time that night. *I would have chosen you.* A soft knock on the other side of the door brought me back to reality and I rushed forward and threw the locks.

Only then did I hear his footsteps retreat down the stairs.

I leaned against the door and brought my fingers up to my lips. Telling him I wasn't going to wait for him had been nothing but my stupid, stubborn pride. What Blue didn't seem to realize was that I didn't have a choice, either. Not really. Like him, I was already in too deep.

12

Blue

I pulled up to my new "home" and let out a sigh. The place was a dump. Not that I was expecting anything more, but I had been hoping.

The house was the size of a small shoebox. A brick square with a dilapidated roof. It boasted one door and exactly two small windows at the front. There was no driveway, so I parked at the curb and walked through the definitely not mowed grass. A set of partially crumbling concrete steps led to the faded and chipping black door. I used my key to unlock the joke of a lock and walked inside.

It smelled stale in here, like the air hadn't moved since nineteen fifty. I felt around for the light on the wall and flicked it when my hand ran over the switch. Dim lighting flooded the room from the single bulb that looked like someone literally just shoved a glass bulb into the ceiling.

There was a saggy, green plaid couch in the center of the room. A brown wooden coffee table, littered with empty beer bottles, and a leather armchair with a hole in the back set off to the side.

The only nice thing in the room was the TV. Druggies loved their technology. And they also loved video games. A fifty-inch flat screen sat on the black entertainment center directly across from the couch, and beside it sat an Xbox.

Maybe the place wouldn't be so bad after all.

I walked through the door to my right and into a tiny kitchen. The cabinets were pea green, the countertops were laminate made to look like wood, and the fruit-themed wallpaper was peeling off the walls. The fridge was white and appeared to be new. I pulled it open and was hit with the new fridge smell. The inside was clean and cool, with all the appropriate bachelor food: ham, turkey, cheese, mayo, and beer.

I looked around a bit more and found a cabinet filled with a few other staples, like coffee and chips. After my tour of the kitchen, I walked back through the living room and into the bedroom. There was a queen-sized bed with clean white sheets and an old-fashioned quilt covering the top.

The sink in the bathroom was pink. It made me think of Julie and her razor. I hadn't wanted to leave her tonight. When I looked around this place and realized what I gave up to come here, I thought about punching myself in the head.

I heard the front door open and close swiftly and my body went on alert. I creeped out of the bathroom and peered into the living room, my gaze colliding with Slater.

"What the hell are you doing here?"

"Thought I'd stop by and welcome you to the neighborhood," he said.

"You live around here?"

"A couple blocks over."

"Your house as nice as mine?"

He snorted. "Your bathroom sink pink?"

I grinned. "I swear it's like an old lady decorated this place in like the thirties."

Slater grunted and made himself comfortable in my leather chair. That left me with the plaid green monster.

"What the hell happened tonight?" I said, making myself uncomfortable on the couch.

"Besides you beating the crap out of the crew's leader?"

"He deserved it," I said, hard.

Slater inclined his chin. "I won't argue. That was a ballsy move, taking him on like that. Could've backfired."

I knew too well how bad things could have gone earlier. If I had been thinking, I would never have done that. But I wasn't thinking. The minute he started putting his paws all over Julie, my brain left the building.

Lucky for me my little lapse in judgment got me some respect.

"Who is she to you?" Slater asked.

I stared at him stoically. I wasn't bringing Julie into this any more than I already had.

After a few very long silent minutes, Slater chuckled. "Okay, I get it."

"You gonna tell me why you're really working this case?" I said, turning the tables on him.

"What makes you think I'm not here for the same reasons you are?"

"Something tells me you already have more than enough evidence to bring down Dom and some of the crew," I said slowly. "What gives?"

"We both know if we bust them on possession, or even selling, they'll do a couple years, then get out and take up their place right back on the street like they never left."

Unfortunately he was right. "So are you saying you're going to get him on something else?"

"Something that will put him away for a long time. Once he's gone, we can clean house with the drugs."

Had I underestimated Dom earlier tonight? He seemed like such a pansy ass to me. He didn't come off as someone I should be afraid of.

"You going to fill me in?" I asked impatiently.

He sat forward. "Why not? You managed to get some shit out of him tonight that no one else has."

"I did?"

Slater nodded. "You know the member of his crew that's gone? The one he mentioned you could take the place of?"

I nodded.

"I think he killed him."

So we were talking murder. Julie was dancing with a murderer tonight. The thought made me sick inside. "Murder," I said thoughtfully.

"His name was Milo VanMeeter." Slater explained. "Worked with Dom for years, he was his right hand. Then one day he ups and leaves. No one hears from him again. Dom stops mentioning his name. It's like he ceased to exist."

"But he brought him up tonight."

"First time I've ever heard him mention Milo."

"And he said he's never coming back,"
Slater glanced at me. "He killed him. I know it."

"Why would he kill one of his own?"

"Judging from the gossip I hear through the crew, Dom was pissed because he got word that Milo was trying to nudge him out and take over with the supplier. And we both know whoever controls the supply…" He trailed off.

"Controls the job." I finished for him.

Slater sat back and looked at me.

"So where is the supply being funneled from? Where are they hiding it?" I wondered.

"I can't figure it out. I've been working this case for a year. At first I thought it was all happening in Myrtle Beach, but then LeBraun moved some of his crew up here, put Dom in charge, and I realized we'd been looking in the wrong place all this time."

"We'll figure this out," I vowed. It had only been one night and already I was anxious to be done. I wanted to wrap this case so I could get back to real life. Before Julie had the chance to move on completely.

"You need to be careful," Slater said. Something in his voice told me it wasn't a casual warning.

"I'm always careful."

"Dom threatened you tonight."

I shrugged and sat back against the couch. "Maybe I'm just too confident, but his little 'I'll kill you' threat tonight didn't seem all that serious."

Slater's eyes met mine. His gaze was steady and clear. "In the past year, I've never heard him actually threaten someone like he did tonight. Dom doesn't like to get his hands too dirty. He usually has his thugs take care of his business."

"See? No worries," I replied.

"You don't get it. He doesn't make idle threats. According to the gossip, the last person Dom ever verbally threatened was Milo."

And now Milo was suspected as being dead.

I nodded slowly. Being precautious wouldn't hurt. In fact, it would be smart.

"You get under his skin, Gray," Slater said, using my undercover name.

I wondered if he even knew my real name. Hell, I didn't know his.

"He's going to be watching you. He's going to look for a reason to take you down," he said, then studied me for a moment. "You might be just what this case needs."

"Why's that?"

"I have a feeling your presence in the crew is going to stir things up. It's going to push Dom's buttons. Push them enough that something slips."

I felt my lips curve. "Pushing buttons is what I do best."

Slater nodded. "Just be careful how far you push. You don't want to end up like Milo."

A little sliver of fear moved down my spine. I pushed it away. I didn't have time for fear. I needed to focus because the cut-and-dry drug case I thought I was working just turned a little more complicated.

Complicated as in murder.

13

Julie

The next two weeks were like a piece of chewed meat that lay inside someone's gut for days. It slowly rotted away, weighing me down and giving me a bad case of acid reflux.

(Now you see why I don't eat meat.)

I felt Blue's absence like a rash that wouldn't go away. It made me grouchy (can't you tell with all the rotting meat and rash talk?). But what made it worse was that I couldn't understand how I could feel the absence of someone who had never been present in the first place. Yeah, we had one date. It was months ago.

It wasn't even the date I thought of. Not anymore.

It was his kiss. It was the feel of his body against mine. It was that damn lip piercing that I practically yearned to pull through my teeth.

Even though he told me I wouldn't see him around, I still looked for him. Every car that passed by me on the street, I searched the driver's seat. Every man that walked into the salon, my heart would skip and I would seek out his face. When the phone rang, I secretly hoped it was him.

Disappointment was a sour taste in my mouth every single time it wasn't him.

I knew I wouldn't see him. It only made me want to see him more.

I stayed late to restock the display and update my running list for the inventory so I would know what to order next week when I made my call to the suppliers. I took my time. I wasn't really in a hurry to get home anyway. I'd just end up thinking about things—*about a certain person*—I didn't want to think about.

When all the stylists were gone for the day, a still silence blanketed the salon. It was quite the change from the normally bustling atmosphere. Knowing that I'd stalled enough, I made my last notation on my paperwork and then put it away for later. After slinging my bag over my shoulder and grabbing my empty water bottle off the counter, I shut off the lights in the back room and pulled the door around on my way out.

All the stylist chairs were empty and lined up perfectly facing the mirrors. The floors were swept free of hair. A few lights still shone overhead, illuminating the space enough so it wasn't dark.

As I walked from the back of the salon toward the front, I noticed Susan was still in her office. The door was partially ajar and a sliver of light stretched out across the tile floor.

But even if I hadn't noticed the light, I would have known she was still here because her muffled voice caught my attention. Even though I couldn't make out what she was saying, I could hear the tone behind her words… the frustration.

Curious, I crept closer.

(What? You would eavesdrop too and you know it.)

"I told you not to call me here," she ground out, her voice low.

There was a pause as she listened to whoever was on the other end of the line, and then she made a strangled sound. "I told you I would take care of it."

She paused again. I could hear papers ruffling around on her desk.

"There isn't room!" she insisted, and I jumped when a banging sound caught me off guard. It was like she slammed something down on her desk.

Holy moly, I thought I was having a bad day.

"Fine," she snapped. "Let me know when it's taken care of."

The phone slammed down and she blew out a frustrated breath. Like the sneaky gal I was being, I rushed back up the salon and pulled the back room door all the way around so it made a slamming sound. Then I walked down the center of the room, practically stomping my boots so she would hear me coming.

Susan appeared in her office door, a slightly nervous twitch about her. "Julie, I didn't realize you were still here."

I smiled. "Yep, just taking some inventory and restocking the display. I'm all finished now so I'm heading out."

"You were in the back room?"

Duh. That's what I said. "Yeah, I was making notes on my inventory sheet. I restocked the front earlier before everyone left."

"Oh." Susan relaxed. "Well, thank you. You've been doing a wonderful job."

Something about the way she delivered the compliment seemed sad. I couldn't imagine why me being good at my job was a bad thing.

"Is everything okay?" I asked hesitantly. I knew we were friends, but it seemed wrong not to ask.

Susan gave me a bright smile. "Everything's great! Now go on. Get out of here. Have a great night."

I wasn't going to press. She was my boss after all. "You too," I replied and walked toward the front door. "I'll see you tomorrow."

On my way to the car, I wondered about Susan's personal life. I wondered if she had a personal life. It seemed like she was always at the salon, like Razor's Edge was her life.

Of course, I knew it couldn't possibly be the only thing, so it made me ponder what or who Susan spent her time with when she wasn't working.

I thought about it the whole drive home, until I walked into my comfy townhouse and kicked off my boots. I went straight upstairs, avoiding the bed and the memories it now held, and straight for my sweatpants. They were purple, too big and insanely comforting. I pulled them on, knotted the drawstring waist, and then folded the waistband over itself so I didn't trip and fall on my way back downstairs. With my pants, I put on a baggy gray T-shirt with sequins on the pocket and then padded barefoot downstairs.

In the kitchen, I made a huge bowl of popcorn with real melted butter, scrounged around for a box of peanut M&Ms and a bottled water, then carried my haul out into the living room to take up residence on the couch.

Once all my snacks were settled and a fuzzy blanket was waiting on the cushions, I put in my favorite movie, *Pride & Prejudice,* and then settled down for a night of munching and romance.

Thank goodness Mr. Darcy didn't look a thing like Blue.

Sometime during my movie and copious amounts of sugar and butter, I fell asleep curled up inside my blanket. I dreamt about a man with intensely blue eyes, who spoke with an accent and kissed me in the pouring rain. I became extremely irritated when someone started knocking… trying to make my swoon-worthy dream boyfriend pull away from my lips.

I gave a growl and it brought me enough out of sleep to realize I wasn't dreaming the sound. Someone was knocking on my front door.

I jolted up, squinting at the TV and the blue screen, and wondered what time it was. It was completely dark in here except for the light coming from the television. It had to be the middle of the night.

I glanced at the door. Who would be knocking at this hour? I got up, pulling the blanket around my shoulders like a shield, and crept over to the door.

The knocking had stopped.

Leaving the chain across the top, I unlocked the door and pulled it open just enough to see out. Cool night air leaked through the open space and weaved around my bare toes, causing them to curl against the floor.

Someone was retreating down the steps off my tiny porch. He was wearing a black leather jacket and a gray knit cap.

"Blue?" It was more of a whisper than anything. I blinked, wondering if perhaps I was still dreaming.

He stopped but kept his back turned. I didn't have to see his face to know it was him. My heart was practically clawing its way out my chest to get to him. No one else affected me that way. No one.

"I shouldn't have come so late," he said, his voice low.

"I don't care what time it is."

His shoulders slumped, just ever so lightly. I only noticed because everything in me was focused on him. It was almost like he was relieved I opened the door, relieved that I would welcome him inside.

"C'mon. It's cold outside," I told him, trying to open the door wide, but the chain stopped it from moving. I rolled my eyes at myself and closed it, quickly removing the lock. When I reopened the door, I stumbled back a bit because I wasn't expecting Blue to be so close.

He was in the doorframe, his broad chest inches from my face. After recovering from my initial shock from his closeness, I looked up and gasped.

He looked like hell.

14

Blue

A couple weeks since I saw Julie. A couple weeks of slumming with people I really didn't like. Bullshitting and waiting for Dom to really accept me into the crew. I still felt like I was an outsider waiting to be invited into an exclusive clique.

It wasn't a position I reveled in. In fact, I hated it. The real me was the kind of person who didn't necessarily care what other people thought of me. I was never the type to try to fit into a certain crowd or group. I was who I was, and trying to be anything else was a waste of time.

Unfortunately, I couldn't be the real me right now. I had to be Gray. Apparently, Gray was the type of guy who waited around for an invitation.

I could see the logic in that, especially in this line of business. Just like in the corporate world, there was a hierarchy to drugs: the big man who ran the operation, the supplier, the area bosses, and then the minions who worked for them.

But being someone's bitch wasn't my style. It was annoying. It was vaguely pathetic, and I wasn't pathetic. I certainly wasn't going to let Gray be pathetic either.

In the past two weeks, I'd barely made any headway in this case. Things started out strong the night of the club, but after that, Dom didn't really say much. He made no invites, no inquiries. I was certain he asked around about me in Myrtle Beach because Slater told me. He couldn't have been told bad things because he wouldn't tolerate me hanging around with some of the crew and showing up at the clubs they frequented.

So what was the deal?

Push.

Something whispered in the back of my head. The Gray in me said it was a bad idea, but everything else seemed to come up with a badass plan.

The night that went well was the night I acted like Blue. Challenging Dom, getting in his face, using my fists and basically ordering everyone to keep their hands off Julie. He responded to that, to the action, to my hands-on approach.

Sitting around wasn't going to get me anywhere with Dom. Action was the solution, so I climbed into the Mustang and put it in drive.

As far as I could tell, Dom lived alone, but there were always people at his place. There was always more than one female there as well. He lived in a one-story brick house, not really in the heart of the ghetto, but more on the outskirts. In my opinion, he chose that place because it was nicer than what the rest of us had and it made him feel like a king ruling over his subjects. The guy had a major ego problem.

However, his place wasn't so far that he wouldn't be able to keep an eye on what was going down in his neighborhood.

I parked at the curb and got out, jogging across the half-dead lawn, and pounded on the front door. It swung open and one of the crew members, Tony, stood blocking my path.

I motioned with my chin. "What up, Tony?" I said and held my fist out for a pound. He regarded me suspiciously for a moment, but then he returned the pound and motioned for me to enter the house.

Even though it was the middle of the day, the place was shut up like a tomb. Curtains covered the windows, and the only light was from a floor lamp sitting in the corner of the room. Dom was sprawled out on a black leather couch, holding a controller to an Xbox as he and a few guys played some bloody war game on the large flat screen.

No one paid me any attention as I walked into the room, which was filled with marijuana smoke, and the scent made my nostrils burn. How anyone smoked that shit was beyond me. There were a bunch of open forty containers on the coffee table, and I held back a snort. Nothing like getting drunk and high in the middle of the day instead of actually getting a real job. One that didn't kill people with overdoses.

"What's up, Dom?" I said, stopping behind the couch and pretending interest in the Xbox game.

He ignored me.

A flash of irritation slapped my insides. I had enough of this shit. I worked on this case for months in Myrtle Beach and we got nowhere. I came home, thinking I could finally get my life back. I got a second chance with Julie, and then this case got in the way again.

I stalked around the couch and across the room, toward the game console. With a very angry and deliberate jerk, I yanked the cord from the wall. The TV screen turned blue as the game system shut off.

The silence in the room was deafening.

I could feel the anger wafting off Dom. "What the hell!" he roared, throwing the controller down, and it bounced off the coffee table and hit the floor. He jolted to his feet, an angry set to his jaw and fisted hands at his side. "You trying to piss me off?"

"I'm tired of waiting around," I replied.

"Excuse me?"

Everyone in the room sat tense and waiting to see what Dom would do.

"You said there was an opening in the crew. You said you were going to check me out, give me a position. That was weeks ago. I'm tired of waiting. I need to get paid."

He regarded me stonily for several minutes. I held my ground. Shit, I would love for him to charge me. I was up for a fight. Frustration simmered just underneath my skin, and the more time that passed, the harder and harder it was getting to contain it.

"I checked you out," he said, offering no other explanation.

"Well, then I know damn well you know I'm qualified."

"You're qualified." He allowed.

"Then what the fuck, Dom? You trying to jerk me around? You want to see how far you can push me?"

He crossed his arms over his chest. He looked stupid in his way-too-baggy shorts and too-big designer white tee. I would never understand the trend to wear a baseball hat crooked either. It looked stupid.

"The crew in Myrtle Beach might trust you. But I don't." His eyes narrowed as he spoke.

"Isn't LeBraun your boss? Are you saying what's good enough for him ain't good enough for you?"

A couple guys who'd been reclining against the couch jumped to their feet. Dom held up his hand like he was telling them to stand down. I wanted to roll my eyes.

"This is my territory," Dom began. "And I run it how I see fit. If I don't trust you, then I don't trust you."

"So that's it, then? I'm out?" I kept a lid on my cool. Showing how upsetting this was wouldn't be good. Mentally, I was kicking myself. This could end badly. I could blow everything I'd been setting up. This could be a real setback for the case. Watson would have a shit fit if I told him I pissed off the crew here.

Maybe I should have listened to Gray on this one instead of listening to what my gut was telling me.

When Dom didn't say anything else, I muttered a nasty expletive and then stalked to the door.

"Gray," Dom said before I got there.

I stopped. "What?" I spat.

"You want my trust? You gotta earn it."

Boo-yah! I mentally high-fived myself. I was kickass.

"How do you want me to do that?" I asked, trying to sound like I was bored.

"Do a job for me."

My stomach revolted. Selling drugs to people wasn't what I wanted to do. Yes, it was part of a bigger plan to get those drugs off the street, but selling them to anyone and adding to the problem I was trying to clean up felt wrong.

But I would do it if I had to.

"What kind of job?"

"I got a shipment that needs to be delivered to Myrtle Beach."

Something inside me relaxed, and I swung to face Dom. "You want me to deliver it?"

I could set up a sting. I could confiscate the drugs and we could take them all down for trafficking. This was good. Real good.

"No," Dom said, cutting into my mental happy dance.

Well, damn. "Then what?"

"I need a delivery vehicle—one that won't look shady—to transport the shipment. Something that won't catch the eye of the po-po."

Po-po = police.

"Everyone in this room has a car." I pointed out. "I'll drive it down in my Mustang."

"You ain't got enough room in your backseat for the goods," he said.

I perked up a little. So this was a major haul. These assholes were going away for a long time.

"We don't use crew cars for this shit, man. The less connected we are the better."

"So you want me to steal something," I said, understanding what he was getting at.

"You do that. Do it without getting caught, and I'll let you make the delivery."

Slater, who'd been making out with some blonde in the corner until this point, looked up. I ignored the fact he was looking at me. I wondered what he was thinking.

"You gonna pay me for the delivery?"

Dom smiled. It was a cold and calculating smile. "You'll get a cut."

"Consider it done."

"Gray," Dom said.

I looked back.

"Don't fuck this up. I only give one shot."

Little did he know this was my one shot to take him down, and one shot was all I was gonna need. "I'll be back in a couple hours."

Dom seemed surprised. "You're doing it now?"

"Time is money," I said.

"Slater, go with him." Dom ordered. "Watch him."

Slater untangled himself from the blonde and followed me out the door. We didn't speak until we were both shut in my Mustang and pulling away from the house. Slater glanced at me with a smirk. "Tired of waiting around?"

"Fuck," I said. "I don't know how you do this shit. How long you been under?"

"I stopped counting a long time ago," he said, low. Something about the way he said it made me wonder how much of himself he'd lost along the way.

"One shot," I said, bringing us back to the topic at hand.

"Better make it good."

"I can do better than good," I said and pulled out my cell phone I used when I needed to contact the department. I hit a button and a few minutes later spoke into the other line. "It's Markson," I said when Watson picked up his end.

Slater looked at me and smiled.

"I need a tow truck and a junker on the back of it," I told Watson.

"Where?" he said, not bothering to ask me too many questions. He would never ask me unless the situation was dire. He had no way of knowing who was within earshot and what angle I was working.

I rattled off the name of a street across town.

"I'll have it there in an hour." Watson confirmed.

I hung up. "We got an hour. Want to grab something to eat?"

Slater laughed. "Hell yeah."

I drove to the nearest drive-through and pulled into the line.

"A tow truck?" Slater asked.

I nodded. "I figured I could sell it to Dom as being cop proof. Cops don't usually look twice at tow trucks on the interstate. Those guys are just doing their jobs, hauling damaged cars to the junkyards and service centers."

"The supply can go inside the car its hauling," Slater said, nodding.

"Exactly. Keeps it out of the cab with the driver. Plus," I added as I drove one car length forward, "it will just look cool I had enough balls to 'steal' a frickin' tow truck in the middle of the day."

"What would you have done if Dom had sent someone besides me with you?" Slater asked.

I smiled. "I would have really stolen something."

We ordered our food and drove to the location I told Watson. While we waited, we ate. Watson was true to his word and about an hour later, someone pulled up in a tow truck with a four-door sedan loaded on the back. The man driving parked it and then got out and jogged to the idling car waiting behind him.

The men drove off in the direction they came from, leaving Slater and me alone with the truck.

"I'll drive it back to Dom's. You drive this."

I made a move to get out of the car when Slater stopped me. "I hate to rain on your parade here, but I got to warn you."

"About what?"

"The last time anyone saw Milo was when he was doing a run for Dom."

"You saying Dom's gonna kill me after I deliver the supply?" Julie's face flashed before my eyes and my insides turned to ice.

"I'm saying having a guy disappear after a job is an awfully convenient way to get rid of them and not have to pay them their cut."

It was obvious Dom didn't like me. He didn't trust me. He thought I would fail today. He certainly wasn't expecting me to show up barely two hours after he issued me a challenge.

I started to doubt the way I handled this. Should I have acted like this job of proving myself was harder? Should I have acted like I wasn't quite as good at this?

The burger I just ate sat in my stomach like a boulder. It was too late now. I had the tow truck, the junker to keep the supplies in, and a plan. Slater would keep his mouth shut about how I got the car, and I would get the job of delivering the supplies.

I wasn't going to worry about what would happen to me after the job was done because I planned to set up a sting and bust these assholes before any of them had the chance to try and kill me.

I felt better after thinking about it. The burger I ate went back to digesting, and I gave Slater a level stare. "I appreciate you telling me that."

"I don't want to see you die. Sometimes I wonder why the hell the good guys even try anymore."

Being undercover for so long had turned Slater bitter. I needed to end this case, not just for me, but for him too. I had a bad feeling that if this case didn't wrap, he was going to end up shifting alliances.

"We're gonna get him, man," I said confidently.

Slater nodded.

"See you at Dom's."

"Be careful," Slater said before I shut the door and jogged away.

15

Julie

I was wearing purple sweatpants. Oversized purple sweatpants. My butt probably looked like a swollen raisin.

Check out the swollen ass on that chick, said NO man ever.

"Is everything okay?" I asked as I backed up toward the sofa, refusing to turn around and give him the worst view of his life. Suddenly my favorite sweatpants seemed like the top contender for the next time I made a donation to the Salvation Army.

But even my careful way of walking didn't stop him from roving his eyes over my entire body. Beneath my T-shirt, I felt my nipples pull taut with need. Well, damn. I wasn't wearing a bra. I resisted the urge to cross my arms over my chest and dove onto the couch, yanking the blanket over my purple lower half and holding it against my chest.

"You weren't in bed?" he asked, stepping around the sofa into my line of sight.

I shook my head. "I was watching a movie."

He glanced at the blue screen on the flat screen. "Looks entertaining."

"I fell asleep," I said, sheepish.

"Your hair is messy." He pointed out, lazily unzipping his leather jacket.

My pulse started pounding. I told myself it was because he insulted me and I was mad. I was about to snap some really good comeback, but words failed me when the jacket slid off his arms and he tossed it onto a chair nearby. Then he yanked the gray cap from his head and tossed it beside his jacket.

My hands tightened around the blanket I was using to shield myself. I almost laughed out loud because there wasn't a shield in this entire universe that would protect me from the freaking sexiness he exuded.

Ripped jeans dipped low on his abdomen, so low that I knew just the slightest lift of his arms would reveal to me his flat, hard stomach and the waistband of his boxers. The long-sleeved T-shirt he was wearing molded to his body, almost like it suffered from static cling.

But I knew better.

If I were that shirt I would caress every last inch of his skin I could.

The silver ring in his lower lip taunted me, and if it weren't for his amazing body, I wouldn't be able to take my eyes off the piercing.

I had no idea I was such a lustful ho. Until I met Blue.

"Your eyes are still a little fuzzy from sleep." He observed, stepping closer to the couch. His voice turned husky, like he knew my eyes weren't fuzzy from sleep—like he knew it was desire he provoked within me.

When I didn't say anything, he stopped, his legs coming up against the couch. "You got room over there for me?"

My stomach quivered with nervous excitement, and I involuntarily squeezed my thighs together with anticipation. Slowly, I lifted up the blanket, inviting him close, peaking up at him from beneath my lashes.

Even though the couch was sizable, he sat so close that his entire side and hip brushed up against me. I imagined it was a lot like the feeling of sticking your finger in a light socket. My entire body was zapped with energy and it rippled all the way down to my bare toes.

"I like your pants," he said, a grin curving his lips.

I felt my cheeks heat with embarrassment. "I wasn't expecting anyone."

"I've wondered," he murmured, turning his head so he could look at me fully.

"About what?"

"About what you did when no one was looking." He tucked a stand of blond hair behind my ear. "How you dressed." He reached between us and grabbed a wayward piece of popcorn. "What you eat, what you do…"

I swallowed thickly. That implied he thought about me. *A lot.*

"It's not very exciting."

"Everything about you excites me."

"Is this a booty call?" I blurted out. I felt my own eyes widen after I heard the words that just shoved their way out of my mouth.

He threw back his head and laughed. I stared at the perfect rows of white teeth in his mouth. He had a sexy laugh: throaty and deep. "Could this even be considered a booty call if I've never had any of that purple booty?"

Oh, God. Did he get a glimpse of my purple rear end when I wasn't looking?

My face flamed with mortification. I wanted to yank the blanket over my head and disappear. I sounded completely arrogant just now, implying that I was so irresistible that he would come here in the middle of the night just for some action.

It reminded me that he never actually told me why he was here.

"You're cute when you're flustered." Blue teased.

"Is everything okay?" I asked, concern pushing back the embarrassment I suffered.

"Everything's fine," he said, stretching his arm out along the back of the couch. I resisted the urge to rest my head against it.

"You're sure?" I asked, scrutinizing his face, looking for even a hint of doubt.

He nodded. "It's been a long week. I needed a break."

The weariness I first sensed when I opened the door reappeared. He did seem tired. Working undercover had to be taxing. It was a twenty-four-hour job. He never got a break.

I tilted my head to the side and studied him. "Do the lines ever get blurry?" I asked thoughtfully.

"Blurry how?"

"Between the good and the bad. Between Blue and Gray. It seems like pretending to be someone else all the time could be dangerous. It could make you forget who you really are."

"I guess sometimes, yeah," he replied. "Sometimes people commit crimes for reasons they think are honorable. It doesn't make it right… but I understand it."

I nodded. "What about you?" I whispered. "How do you keep track of who you are?"

Blue's gaze was penetrating. The unfathomable color of his stare was so intent and measuring that my chest tightened. It was almost as if he were stripping me bare. Not stripping away my clothes or thinking about me in that way… but looking past the way I looked, past the sexual tension that hummed around us like he was looking for something specific, something that would determine his answer.

Based on the answer he gave, I would wholly assume that he found whatever he was searching for.

His voice practically became my oxygen. I breathed him in. His voice. His presence. His words. "Sometimes it does get hard. Like when I'm surrounded by people who have their own specific code for life, one that I don't understand. Or when it's really late and I'm really tired and it's so dark in my room the only thing I can do is think. Sometimes my thoughts blur… and I can't tell who is Blue and who is Gray."

"How do you figure it out?"

"I think about you."

Everything around me ceased. There was nothing. Nothing but those four words.

"I call up the memory of your laugh. I think about your hair and how it always looks like you just crawled out of bed. I pretend it was my bed and I'm the one who made your hair look like that. I remember how you felt in my arms that night we danced in the rain and how I thought I had finally found someone I never wanted to let go of."

My chest felt tight. Physically tight. It was hard to breathe because so much emotion welled up inside me.

"Do you know why I picked the name Gray, Julie?"

"Because you were going with a color theme?" I squeaked.

He flashed a quick smile and shook his head. His arm stretched between us and the pad of his thumb stroked along my cheekbone and curved beneath my eye, slightly tickling the fringe of bottom lashes. "Because that night after our date… the only thing I could think about were your eyes. The color of a cloudy sky on a winter's day."

He named himself after my eyes.

He named himself after my eyes.

I pinched myself in the arm. Hard. When I winced, Blue frowned. "What did you do that for?" he asked, snatching up my arm and studying the red welt.

"Because I sure as hell must be dreaming." Guys didn't say things like this in real life.

He threw back his head and laughed. He looked back at me, a twinkle in his eye. "Did you wake up?"

I shook my head. Butterflies were swirling around inside me like a mini tornado, sweeping everything around and causing my head to spin.

"Maybe this will help," he said and swooped in.

The arm lying across the back of the couch came forward and his hand gripped the back of my neck.

He leaned forward, crowding my personal space and bringing his face so near that I could feel the warmth of his breath against my lips.

Before I could adjust to the overwhelming closeness, his lips claimed mine. The kiss was urgent and demanding—like he'd been holding back for too long and just couldn't stand another second. I gripped his shirt in my palms and yanked him closer, crushing my lips against his. He kissed with fevered ferocity that lit fire to my blood and caused the inner muscles deep inside me to clench so tightly they began to quiver.

Moisture slicked my crotch, coating my secret place with a lubricant that would welcome his body as part of mine. I groaned, the feeling of my body readying itself for him was almost too much.

His tongue swept between my lips, sliding over my teeth and then delving deep into the confines of my mouth. Our tongues circled lazily, the slightly rough textures of them rubbing together, creating sparks of friction that ran along my nerve endings and threatened to sizzle my brain.

I opened my knees and scooted closer, he wound his arms around my back and yanked me forward. I came up against him abruptly, but our kiss never broke. The second I felt his body against mine, I started moving, my hips grinding against his middle, searching—*no, demanding*—everything he had to give.

The throbbing erection between his legs brushed against the pulsing lips of my vagina, and a sharp moan bubbled up my throat.

Blue tore his mouth away and looked at me. His lips were glistening with moisture and slightly swollen from the intensity of our kiss. "This was *not* a booty call," he insisted.

"Can it be?" I asked, thrusting my hips against him once more.

His hand tightened in a fist at my back and a shudder of pleasure rolled through his limbs. But then his body stiffened and he pinned me with a stare. "No."

Well, that's how I knew I wasn't dreaming. Because if this were an actual dream of mine, he'd already be ripping off my shirt and ravishing my flesh.

I felt my nose wrinkle in obvious distaste. "No?"

"This cannot be a booty call."

"Why the hell not?" I demanded. How dare he come over here looking all hot and bothered, whipping me up into a frenzy of desire, and then turn me down?

He set me away from him and stood. The way his manhood strained against his jeans told me clearly at least part of him wanted me. With a single tug, Blue yanked the blanket away from me and carried it over on the other side of the coffee table, right in front of the darkened fireplace.

He stretched the blanket out on the floor and then bent down (yes, I checked out his ass) and flipped on the little switch, causing a fire to ignite inside the hearth. When he straightened, he clicked the nearby remote and the television turned off, leaving flickering orange flames the only light in the room.

He prowled over to me. I almost forgot to be offended he just turned me down. When he reached out a hand to me, I snatched mine away. "I thought you were leaving."

"I'm not going anywhere," Blue intoned. It sounded like the most delicious threat I'd ever heard.

Maybe I was slow… but he did just turn me down. Right?

After he pulled me to my feet, he reached for the hem of my T-shirt. "What are you doing?" I asked.

A slow smile curved his lips. "I'm going to lay you down over there," he whispered as he lifted my shirt up, "and I'm going to make love to you."

The shirt cleared my head and hit the couch. Cool air brushed over my bare skin as he reached out and palmed my breasts.

I didn't say anything. I couldn't. Just the feel of his fingers caressing the sensitive flesh of my breasts made me bite my lower lip in anticipation.

"You see, Julie," he murmured, lowering his face so his lips grazed my collarbone, "this isn't a booty call. A booty call implies I only want one thing from you."

His lips brushed my skin.

My head fell back.

More kisses trailed up my neck.

"And I want way more than just sex from you." his teeth closed over my earlobe and the cool metal of the piercing shocked my skin.

I gasped. *Damn, he's good.* So good that I was utterly certain I was going to be giving Blue whatever it was he wanted.

16

Blue

I didn't come here for this.

For sex.

But her unapologetic longing wasn't something I was going to deny. I mean, damn. She wanted it. I sure as hell wanted it.

I was going to give it to her.

And after tonight, she wasn't even going to want to look at another man for as long as she lived.

Maybe that was unfair of me to do. Technically, I wasn't available. Technically, I belonged to the job.

Technically, I didn't give a rat's ass.

Her soft probing questions about blurred lines and how I kept track of the real me sort of broke my resolve. Shit, I freaking picked my undercover name based on the color of her eyes. When I was starting to feel weighed down by the world, I thought about her. Everything I said to her was true. I meant every damn, sappy word. Maybe I'd been fooling myself up until this point. Maybe I thought that I had a choice in whether or not she was part of my life.

But I didn't.

She was already a part of my life.

I didn't want to fight how I felt about her anymore.

Not tonight.

I had no clue what tomorrow would bring. I wanted this, these moments. I wanted to show her the way she'd impacted my life since that morning I pulled over her speedy ass.

The skin beneath my touch was supple and the weight in each breast perfectly fit in my palms. I watched her face as I drew my thumbs across her soft nipples and enjoyed the way her eyes flared and the skin drew into fine pebbles beneath my touch. Using a thumb and forefinger, I rolled the little knobs around, tugging on them until she groaned deeply in her throat.

Julie's hands came up and gripped my forearms, so I pinched at her, knowing it was shooting fissures of pleasure right down into her waiting vagina.

This wasn't going to be a quickie. This wasn't going to be me slipping a part of me into her. I was going to take my time. I was going to get to know every last inch of her body the way I'd craved since the moment my eyes met hers.

Reluctantly, I released her breasts and took her hand, leading her around the coffee table and over toward the blanket laid out on the floor. The fire threw off a cozy warmth, combating the chill in the air outside, and cast a smoldering hue around the room.

Pulling Julie around so she was standing with her back to the blanket and her chest to mine, I reached between us for the drawstring on her sweats. One firm tug loosened the fabric and I slid my hands— one on each hip—into the waistband.

Before sliding them down, I paused to look at her. "Say yes," I told her. "Say yes to all the things I'm about to do to you."

"Yes."

It was immediate. It was absolute. It was my new favorite word.

The pants were gone in a matter of seconds. Julie kicked them away and reached for my shirt. Her eager hands slid up beneath the fabric and caressed my sides. Using one hand, I yanked the shirt over my head, dropping it to the floor.

She slid her palms around to the small of my back and stepped forward, lowering her head to take one of my nipples into her mouth. My entire body jerked when her moist, hot mouth closed around me.

My fingers knotted in her hair and held her still while she lapped at my chest with unrelenting passion. All the blood in my body drained to one place and my penis grew so hard that I thought it might pop a hole in my jeans.

When Julie's lips started to venture lower, I pulled her back. "No, you don't," I told her. Quickly, I swept her up and onto her back, laying her out across the blanket like she was my own personal all-you-can-eat buffet.

The scrap of lace and cotton that covered the juncture of her thighs teased me with what lay beneath.

I came over her, holding my weight on my palms, enjoying the way she fit perfectly beneath me. Her hands went back to rubbing all over my chest and occasionally flirting with the waistband of my jeans.

I lowered my face close enough to kiss her, but before I could, she sucked the piercing into her mouth and laved at it with her naughty little tongue. I used to hate this hunk of metal in my face, but damned if I didn't change my mind. There was just a hint of pain when she tugged it a little too hard and it mixed so perfectly with the passion flowing through my veins. It was like without realizing it, she somehow mixed up the perfect tonic of pleasure and pain.

When she was done, she lay back with a contended sigh.

It was the perfect opportunity to swoop in and begin my onslaught of passion. Wedging my nose in that vulnerable soft spot between her ear and jaw, my tongue licked out, wetting the skin before I gently blew my breath over the moist spot.

The little groan she rewarded me with caused a smile to play on my lips as I trailed lingering, hot kisses down the side of her neck and across her chest. Her skin was so smooth. If it weren't warm from the blood that beat beneath its surface, I would have thought it marble.

So entranced by the feel of her against me, I turned my lips and brushed the side of my jaw against her, the roughness of my stubble creating friction between us.

Her body moved restlessly beneath me. She wiggled her hips and used her hands to explore my body, to try and pull me closer. Finally, I gave in. I lowered so my weight pinned her to the floor and halted her movements. She was now completely at my whim.

I liked the power. I liked the feeling of knowing she would likely let me do anything to her because she trusted I would keep her safe. I pinned her arms above her head, using one hand to anchor them against the softness of the blanket.

Even though I held her down, she still found a way to touch me, to participate in what we were doing. Her bare leg came up to wrap around the back of my thigh and pressed my jean-covered cock right against the tender junction of her thighs.

A throaty laugh worked its way out of me. She was naughty. "You're gonna get punished for that," I promised right before I closed my lips over her nipple.

She gasped and tried to arch up off the floor, baring even more of her pliant flesh. I sucked deeply, taking in as much of her as I could and rolling her fullness around the interior of my mouth. I worked at her breast until it became heavy with need and she was begging for more. Then I moved to the other one, scraping my teeth over her nipple and using my free hand to gently grip her mound and bring it closer to my lips.

She tasted like peaches, sweet and creamy. I couldn't get enough of the way she felt in my mouth.

After I released her breasts, I kissed beneath them, sucking small mounds of flesh into my mouth and pulling at them. I didn't do it hard, but in the back of my mind, I hoped she was left with at least one mark on her flesh. I wanted to brand her. I wanted to stake my claim. Every time she looked in the mirror, I wanted her to remember what it was like for my mouth to be on her skin.

"Harder," she urged as if reading my mind.

I obliged, trying not to cause her pain, but giving her what we both wanted. She was a vocal lover, making little mewling sounds, little moans, and gripping my hand with hers where I pinned them.

Inside my jeans, my cock throbbed. It begged for release. Never in my life had I been so ready to slide inside someone as I was right now. I wanted to pound away in her. I wanted to lose myself inside her taut, wet heat.

Anxious to go lower, I glanced up, catching her eyes, and said, "Keep those hands right where they are."

She nodded and bit her lower lip. I removed my hand and moved lower, grasping the fabric of her panties with my teeth and sliding them down her legs. Once they were gone, her legs parted unabashedly and the heady scent of her damp juices was like a siren, like I was a boat, lost at sea, and I was finally coming upon my port.

I sat back on my haunches, splaying my hands out on each of her inner thighs and just looking at the display before me. Perfect pink folds were nestled beneath short, dark silken curls. The passion she felt was clearly visible. She was swollen and throbbing, slick with lubricant.

The engorged button partially concealed by her other tender parts was shiny and heavy. Slowly, I climbed my fingers closer. She sighed and mumbled something neither of us understood. Using my fingers, I parted her folds and caught sight of the depths of her body.

Using a single finger, I swirled just the tip in her wetness and then traced a circle around her, spreading the juice wherever I could. I liked seeing her drip for me. I liked knowing her body was readying itself for me to enter.

Unable to take another second, I delved my finger deep within. She cried out and her legs began to quiver. I worked my finger out and then slid it back in, this time adding another so I was using two to penetrate her body.

The muscles of her vagina squeezed around my fingers and my cock jerked. Keeping my fingers inside, moving at a steady rhythm, I lowered my face and drew the swollen clit into my mouth. I sucked it gently, licking at it with my tongue.

When her thighs pressed in around my head and she started panting, I pulled away. She made a little helpless sound that I found endearing.

Julie reached between us and grabbed my face on either side, pulling me up so she could look into my face. "I want more, Blue."

She released me and sat up as I sat back. Her hands were on my pants in seconds, fumbling with shaky fingers until I sprang free and pointed directly at her. She didn't bother with my jeans; she had what she wanted and her lips slid down over me before I was prepared.

A long shudder moved through my body, and my head fell back. The heat of the fire warmed the side of my body, and colors exploded behind my closed eyes.

She worked me with her hands and mouth as I knelt between her legs. I fumbled with my pants, yanking out a condom from my back pocket and then shoving the jeans down my thighs and pulling her up to take her mouth with mine while I kicked the pants off the rest of the way.

I used the weight of my body to guide her back onto the floor, and her hands clutched my backside, urging me to the center of her body.

"Wait a minute, sweetness," I murmured, pulling back so I could hurry to smooth the condom over my twitching length.

Once it was on, I rested my elbows on either side of her head and held myself just inches above her. She looked up, her eyes heavy with need, but there was more than that. It was almost as if she were slightly in awe of the feelings churning between us.

It was almost overwhelming. This moment had been in the making from the instant I leaned down into her window. The sexual tension, the immediate attraction I felt for her was unlike anything I ever experienced.

It's exactly why this wasn't a booty call.

Julie was never going to be someone that could satisfy me with a late-night call and an hour in the sack. The minute I dipped into her, I was going to be lost.

Her hand came up and cupped the side of my face; her other hand wound around my waist and her little fingers curled against my skin.

The same exact second I joined our lips, I thrust inside her in a single, long, hard thrust.

The kiss broke because both of us moaned. Our lips vibrated with the force of the sound. I held still, feeling her walls stretch out around me, letting the sheer bliss of being inside wash over us both.

She was the first to move, a slight rock of her hips, and then she was patting me on the bottom, giving me instructions to go.

I braced myself on my hands and started to move. Every single thrust sent energy soaring over my nerve endings, prickling over my scalp and making my bones tremble.

Her inner walls spasmed with every plunge, and she moaned, tossing her head back and forth as she clawed at the skin around my waist. Julie began to move, wrapping her hands around my biceps, planting her feet into the floor and raising her pelvis so she could meet each of my thrusts with her own.

It was freaking epic that I stopped moving all together, but the sensation continued on and on and on. I held myself suspended as she worked my rod like no one before. The way she bucked against me, grinding down and milking every ounce of hardness I could give.

Julie collapsed against the blanket, giving me a shy smile before her eyes drifted closed, and I noted the sheen of sweat glistening over her body.

I started to move, swirling around inside her with a swivel of my hips. Her hands knotted in the blanket as I slid one of my palms beneath the small of her back and tilted her lower half upward.

I dove in so deeply that she cried out. Our pelvises were touching and I bore down on her and started to rock. Her little moans turned into a whispered plea, and I felt the exact moment she fell over the edge because she pulled me with her.

Together we spiraled into a passion-laden freefall as the orgasm tore me up from the inside out.

"Blue," she moaned, saying my name over and over again.

When the last tremor of pleasure rippled through me, I collapsed onto the floor, rolling beside her and scooping her into my arms, fitting her against my side. Our skin slid against each other, slick with sweat.

I pressed a kiss to her damp forehead and she sighed.

Sex with her was quite literally the best I ever had. It was almost bittersweet. Sweet because I felt like my body had searched for that kind of closeness, that kind of release since I figured out girls didn't have cooties. And bitter… bitter because it took me so long to experience Julie, bitter because I wanted more… and bitter because after tonight, I might never see her again.

17

Julie

He stayed until darkness began to give way to a shadow-filled sky. We lay by the fire for as long as we could, not really talking.

Okay, we couldn't talk.

Because we were making out like teenagers.

I knew when he was going to leave by the way tension slowly creeped into his body and invaded our moment. I didn't ask him to stay. I knew he couldn't. I didn't tell him I would miss him, even though I would. And I didn't pout because pouting never changed anything.

Instead, I pulled on his shirt (it smelled just like him) and padded barefoot into the kitchen and hit brew on my coffee pot. The rich, deep smell of brewing coffee filled the kitchen as strong arms wrapped around my midsection, pulling me against his hard body.

"You in the habit of drinking joe in the middle of the night?"

"It's for you," I said, enjoying the husky tone to my voice. My body had never felt so liquid, so loved. "It's cold out and I don't like the idea of you out there driving at this hour."

He spun me around and pinned me up against the counter, fitting a muscular thigh between my legs. "I don't want you worrying about me," Blue said seriously.

I didn't bother telling him I wouldn't worry. I wasn't into lying. "How long until I see you again?"

He let out a long sigh and cupped my face in his palms. "I don't know."

I kissed him.

We kissed until the coffee beeped and made its final brewing sounds. I pulled away to fill a stainless steel travel mug almost to the top. I glanced over my shoulder. "Cream?"

"If you have it."

I pulled out a bottle of Vanilla Fire creamer and added a healthy dollop. Using a butter knife, I swirled the coffee and cream together as the fragrant steam hit me in the face. I was so getting up early enough to have coffee in the morning. I was going to need it after spending half the night awake in his arms.

After I deposited the knife in the sink and screwed on the lid, I turned, extending the brew to Blue. He took it and set it on the counter beside us and drew me into a hug, locking his arms around me.

My cheek fit perfectly in the little indentation between his pecs, and I dipped my fingers into the waistband of his jeans. Something shifted around us. It was a feeling, an instinct perhaps. It was as if all of a sudden, a dark cloud drifted right above us, threatening to dampen us with rain.

"Blue?" I asked, not sure how to voice what I was feeling.

"It's going to be okay."

"What is?" I asked, pulling back to search his face.

He picked up the coffee and took a sip, sighing as he swallowed. I knew the coffee was good, but I also knew he was merely stalling.

I wasn't going to like what he was implying. It had to be about his job. The case was heating up. Why else would he come over here in the middle of the night?

The last time he came here, it was because he said he couldn't stand the thought of me out there hating him. He'd said I wouldn't see him again. He did imply that perhaps once the case was over, he and I might have a chance.

But then he showed up tonight. He did things to my body I would crave until my last moments on Earth. He came even after he said he wouldn't. Almost as if he thought it might be his last chance to see me...

Horror streaked through me.

My eyes shot up to meet his grim gaze. "You have a very expressive face," he said.

I slapped my palm against his chest. "You're a jerk." I pushed away from him, going back out into the living room where I stood staring down at the blanket where we'd just made love.

"It isn't as bad as you're thinking," he said softly behind me.

"No?" I asked, tilting my head and staring into the flames. "So you didn't come here tonight as some sort of good-bye?"

He snatched me by the elbow and spun me around. His face pushed close to mine and his blue eyes sparked with anger. "Do you think after that— *after us*—that I wouldn't do every last thing in my power to come back to you?"

"But before we did that?" I challenged.

He swore and released me. I swallowed past the sob threatening to rip its way out of my throat.

"The case is heating up. There's some stuff coming up I gotta do."

"What kind of stuff?"

"You know I can't tell you."

"But it's dangerous?"

"Isn't everything?" he quipped, but I heard the masked wariness deep in his voice.

I dropped onto the sofa, tucking my knees beneath me. It was pointless to ask questions or demand answers. I wasn't about to compromise his cover, his very life, by prying answers out of him.

This was totally out of my area of expertise. I knew color. I knew cut. I knew the best kind of blow dryer and flat iron to buy. Drugs and police work? Not so much.

After a few quiet minutes, he dropped onto the couch beside me, once again laying his arm out across the back of the cushions. "Look, if everything goes well, then there'll be a break in the case very soon. I could have this wrapped up in a couple of weeks."

"That soon?" I glanced at him, hopeful.

His eyes softened and he brushed a strand of hair out of my face. "That soon."

I nodded and gave him a small smile. With a sigh, he got up off the couch and paced near the fireplace. "I just need to know where they're coming from."

"Who?" I asked.

He seemed to realize he spoke out loud and spun. "No one. I really have to go."

I nodded. "Yeah."

I stood up and he looked at his shirt hanging off my frame.

"I'm not giving it back."

He chuckled and grabbed his jacket, sliding it over the sinew of his muscles. "I like the thought of you sleeping in my shirt."

He tugged the gray cap over his mussed short hair and then picked up the coffee. "Thanks for this." He gestured toward the mug.

We walked over to the door, a heavy feeling replacing the light one I felt earlier. Just because I knew he had to go didn't make it any easier.

He undid the locks and turned to glance at me.

"Be careful, okay?" I asked softly.

He wrapped one strong arm around my waist and lifted me off my feet. Holding me tightly, he kissed me. He tasted like coffee, strong and sweet with just a little hint of heat. I pulled his lower lip into my mouth, tasting him to the absolute fullest.

With a deep growl, he pulled back and set me on my feet. "Damn, woman."

I smiled.

When he opened the door, a little bit of my smile slipped as he stepped outside. Leaning back in, he pressed a quick kiss to the tip of my nose. "I'll see ya later, sweetness."

"See ya," I said, softly shutting and locking the door behind him.

I listened for his retreating footsteps until I couldn't hear them anymore. I picked up the blanket off the floor and wrapped it around my shoulders. I didn't bother going up the stairs to bed, instead lying down on the couch, tucking the softness around me.

As I drifted to sleep with the feel of his shirt on my skin, I hoped I would see him again soon.

18

Blue

The interior of the Mustang was a lot colder than the inside of Julie's living room, but I didn't really feel the chill. My blood was still sizzling from what we just did. Fuck, she was one hot woman.

I'd never slept with a woman who so actively participated in love making like that. Her hands were everywhere. Her mouth was eager, and her hips… shit, her hips. That woman could for certain be a professional bull rider.

It made me wonder what all the other women I dated had been missing… Surely it wasn't me that had been lacking; surely they just weren't that hot.

It didn't matter anymore. I would never go back to a lukewarm bedmate again. Hell, I never wanted another bedmate.

It dawned on me then that Julie turned the tables on me. It was me who vowed to make her never want another man again, but it was me who didn't so much as want to look at another woman now.

I glanced down at the coffee cup in the cup holder and smiled slightly. She even made damn good coffee.

She was a keeper.

I stared out the windshield at the vacant street (I parked several blocks away from Julie's townhouse) as a bitter taste erupted from the back of my throat. I literally felt my world shift around me.

Clarity was like a bucket of ice water in the face.

I didn't want this life anymore. I didn't want to live for my job. I didn't want to eat, sleep, and breathe this case. Living in a ghetto house with a frickin' pink bathroom was not how I wanted to spend my days. Balancing myself as two separate people with two very different ideas of lifestyle was getting old.

I wanted this case over.

I wanted to be Blue again. I wanted to spend time with Julie. I wanted to drive my sweet-ass Challenger around town and sleep in a bed that didn't have dust mites living in the mattress.

I knew what I was doing was important. I knew what I was doing was absolutely necessary. I couldn't give up, but this case needed to be resolved. People's lives were at risk and on hold.

Dom was pleased when I showed up with the tow truck. He seemed surprised that I thought of such a vehicle for delivery, but he agreed that it made a great cover for what we were really transporting.

In the end, I got the job. I was going to deliver the haul of drugs to Myrtle Beach. He put me on standby. I was to wait for the call, then come running. My job was now to be available. Whenever Dom said drive, I said how far.

I tried to get the address of where the supply was kept, but he clammed up. I didn't want to press the issue because he already didn't like me much. So it was back to waiting. Waiting for the call, for the delivery.

I wasn't too worried about Slater's warning until Dom announced that he would ride with me to Myrtle Beach. That threw a huge wrench in my plans. I was going to have to work something out with Watson in advance for the sting because I wouldn't have as much freedom on the road.

But it wasn't really arresting them that had me worried. We would get the crew. What worried me was the fact Dom wanted to come. My instincts were screaming that the only reason he wanted to ride along was because he had no intention of ever letting me come home.

He would use me for the job, then get rid of me when we were still alone. Then he'd tell the rest of the crew I decided to skip town and not come back. The only one who wouldn't believe him would be Slater, but by then it would be too late.

The more I thought about it, the more I thought about Julie. Odds were I wasn't going to die. My eyes were wide open. We'd take Dom in before he could act, and I would come home. But… But even the best laid plans sometimes got messed up. I didn't want to go into this without seeing Julie at least one more time.

The problem was every time I saw her, things between us got better and better. It took everything I had to walk out her door tonight.

I sipped at the coffee, the rich sweetness settling some of my thoughts, and then I reached under the driver's seat to grab the cell phone Watson gave me to keep in contact when I could. I only talked to them twice since going back undercover.

It rang several times before I heard the line pick up. I had a ping of regret that it was the middle of the night, but Watson knew I would only call when I could.

"Gray," Watson said, his voice thick with sleep. "Is everything okay?"

"Sorry to call at such a late hour, sir." I apologized.

I heard the ruffling of what I assumed were covers and then his voice came on the line, more alert than before.

"Nonsense. Anytime. You have information for me?"

"Not much. I've successfully infiltrated the crew here. I've been asked to deliver a load of drugs into South Carolina within the next few days. I'm hoping I'll be able to see where the drugs are coming from when I make the pick-up."

"That's excellent. Keep me informed. We can set up a sting operation for you to be intercepted on your delivery. We can confiscate the drugs, arrest you, and then you can "roll over" on the others in the crew in exchange for a lighter sentence."

I knew he was speaking hypothetically. I wouldn't actually be charged with anything, but the department would make it look like I was so my secret identity stayed that way. They could make a big deal out of sending me to a facility not in this area so people wouldn't wonder why I wasn't behind bars with the others that I helped put there. Once the ring was busted and dismantled here in town, I could go back to my life, and hopefully no one would be the wiser.

It seemed like a pretty open-and-shut case. Clean. I could do this. I could end this any day now. All I had to do was wait for the call with my delivery schedule.

"There's another reason I called," I said before Watson could hang up the phone. I cleared my throat. "It's—uh—personal."

"Whatever you need," he said. I hoped he would still feel that way after I told him what I needed.

"There's this woman," I began.

"Mother of God, Gray, don't tell me you fell for someone on the crew."

"No. No, nothing like that."

"Thank God. Do you know what kind of compromise that would be to your cover?"

I didn't say anything because even though Julie wasn't on the crew, she was still technically a compromise to my cover.

Watson swore. "What is it, Gray?" he demanded.

"The night I went undercover, I stood up a woman for a date," I began.

"Yeah, I remember."

"Well, I dated her before, months before. Before I went undercover. She showed up at the club my first night under. She… uh… fell in with Dom. I intercepted as he was dragging her off the dance floor. I sent her home."

"So she's connected to your undercover alias. And she knows your real name."

"Yes." I paused. "I told her I was undercover."

I yanked the phone away from my ear just in time to be spared the barrage of expletives that came through the line. When Watson was done cussing at me, I rested the cell back against my ear.

"I know it's against protocol. It couldn't be helped. She assured me she wouldn't breathe a word. She promised if she ever saw me out in town, she would pretend she had no idea who I was."

"You trust this woman?"

"I do, sir. Absolutely."

"That's good enough for me."

"There's something else."

"Jesus, Gray. What!"

"The last guy to deliver for Dom never came back. Dom wants to ride with me. I don't think it's a good sign," I said, letting that sink in. "I want your word, sir, that if something happens to me, she will be notified privately. I don't want her hearing about me on the news. She's important to me. She means something."

Watson was silent on the line for a long time. "You saying you think you're gonna die, Gray?" he asked gruffly.

"I have no intention of dying, sir. But I just… I want to be sure she gets the respect she deserves. She isn't my wife, but…"

"You don't have to explain, son. I understand. You have my word."

The tightness between my shoulder blades seemed to ease a little with his promise. I gave him Julie's name and address and then cut the connection.

After putting the secret cell back where I was hiding it, I put the car in drive and went back to the ghetto.

19

Julie

Twelve. That's how many haircuts I did today. That doesn't count the couple of eyebrow waxes and two highlights I did as well. My fingers were numb from holding the scissors. My feet were growing blisters the size of my head, and my shoulders ached from holding my arms up to work.

I swear every walk-in that came in today was pointed in my direction. But I made a lot of tips and I sold quite a few products, which would mean some extra commission. I couldn't wait to go home to peel the boots off my tired feet, take a long hot bath, and sip a glass of wine.

But first, I had to finish work.

Of course my busiest day on the floor styling hair was also my day to stay late and go through inventory and call the supplier. I thought about putting it off until tomorrow. But tomorrow was Saturday. I wasn't entirely sure if my suppliers were open on Saturdays. I'd always placed my order on a weekday.

Not to mention tomorrow was my day off. After today, I sincerely wanted to sleep half the day away. I'd rather yank my toenails out with a pair of tweezers than get up early and come in here again tomorrow.

Most of the girls were finishing up their day (some had already left) when I peeked out the window at the darkening sky. There was a lot of cloud coverage today; the sky seemed lower than usual, like it was heavy and pressing in on the town. I could see the trees outside swaying in the wind, and I wondered if perhaps a rainstorm was heading our way. Living so close to the coast sometimes made the weather here unpredictable.

Enough stalling, I told myself and headed into the back room where I kept my clipboard and inventory sheets. I did pause to quickly brew myself a mug of coffee with the Kuerig that Susan bought for all the girls last Christmas.

I definitely needed a pick-me-up after today. I felt the beginnings of a monster headache behind my eyes and hoped the caffeine would kick it out of my head. After my coffee was done, I added a splash of creamer from the fridge and carried it over to where I kept my notes.

I glanced at the list and sipped my coffee as I went through the cabinets, double-checking to make sure I had everything listed that the salon would need. I liked to order in bulk. It seemed easier to place one larger order every couple weeks than to constantly be ordering stock.

After making all the notations and double-checking the order, I pulled out my cell to place the call to the distributor. Just before I hit send, I realized I didn't check the display out front. After the busy day we had, I knew we were running low on several products. With a sigh, I set the phone down and took another gulp of coffee. Clipboard and pen in hand, I started out to the front.

The sound of the front doors opening and closing heavily had my footsteps slowing. I wasn't sure why, but the sound… It just seemed different than usual. More forced.

I heard the clicking of Susan's heels on the tile and then her muffled gasp. "What are you doing here?"

I kept just inside the back room, instinctively knowing I shouldn't go out there.

"You haven't been answering your phone," said a voice that seemed vaguely familiar. I tilted my head, trying to decide where I'd heard it before.

"I've been busy," Susan said tightly.

"Busy doing what?"

"I have a business to run," she said, and I swear I heard the hint of fear in her tone. My stomach began to knot, wondering what the hell was going on.

"So do I, and when you don't answer the phone, I start to wonder," the male replied. I heard his footsteps shuffle farther into the room. "Wonder if maybe you're going to turn on me."

"I'm not."

"I'm gonna need to see the product."

"It's safe."

"I want to see."

"What if someone saw you come in here?"

"So?" he challenged. "Everyone needs a haircut from time to time."

The tension coming from out there was thick; I felt it oozing through the doorway, trying to tangle me up in its nasty web.

"It's in the back," Susan finally said. I guess she was going to show him whatever it was he wanted to see.

But wait… I was in the back.

The minute they stepped into this room, they would know that I was eavesdropping. Something told me that wasn't good.

I looked around for a place to hide, my eyes landing on the door to what Susan said was where the water heater and stuff was. I turned to flee, to hide, when the man's voice caught my attention once more.

"Let me remind you," he said, low and menacing. "*You* work for *me*. Those who try to turn on me, who try to venture out on their own… It doesn't end well for them."

A charged silence permeated the air, and I imagined Susan and whoever it was out there locked in a stare-down. It was a good time to get to hiding.

"You killed him, didn't you?" Susan said, accusation thick in her tone.

Wait a minute. I stopped, turned back to the doorway. *Who killed who, now?*

"That's a pretty serious accusation," the man said mildly. Like being accused of murder wasn't that big of a deal.

Who is this guy?

"You told me he was out on a job. No job would last this long. You kept me on a string. You knew when I realized what you did that I wouldn't do this anymore." I could hear the emotion welling up in Susan, like she had some sort of closed valve in her throat and the pressure from what she was feeling was bottling up behind it, ready to explode. "I should have realized sooner." Her voice cracked.

"Listen, bitch." The man breathed. "I don't have time for your moaning. Like I said. *You* work for *me*. Now show me the stuff."

"Get out," she demanded.

Whoa. Props to the boss lady. She had some lady balls. I pumped a fist in the air. *You go, girl.*

"What did you just say?" he practically growled. Little goose bumps prickled my skin at his threatening and dangerous tone.

"I said get. Out. Now."

I heard a sharp slapping sound and Susan cry out.

Eavesdropping was one thing. Listening to a man beat up on a woman was totally different. She wasn't the only one with lady balls.

Taking a deep breath, I slapped the clipboard down on the counter and walked out of the back room, not being subtle at all, clicking the end of my ballpoint pen as I walked.

"Susan," I called like I had no idea she was standing out here. The pair at the other end of the salon froze, surprised, just like I knew they would be. I prepared to act surprised too.

But I didn't have to act.

Shock rippled through me, and it was followed very closely by thick dread. My eyes locked with the man who was arguing with—who just hit—my boss.

I knew him.

I had been warned to stay far, far away.

"Julie," Susan said, a little relief plain in her voice. "I didn't realize you were still here."

I forced my eyes away from the man who made my skin crawl and summoned a fake smile for Susan. "Yep. Still here. I was doing inventory in the back." I cleared my throat. The man's eyes hadn't left me. I knew he recognized me.

After all, I'm the reason he got beat up the night we met.

"I didn't realize you had company." My eyes slid toward the man and then away. "I can finish up tomorrow."

"No need," Susan said quickly. "This gentleman just wanted a haircut. I explained that we already closed for the night."

Susan glanced at him again. "We reopen tomorrow at ten."

He stood there for very long, tense moments. I could see him debating what he should do. Finally, he gave Susan a tight smile. "I'll come back. Tomorrow."

Susan's body tightened.

Dom left. The man Blue warned me about.

He hadn't been here for a haircut. Not at all.

How in the world could Susan know a drug dealer?

20

Blue

Proving myself by "stealing" the tow truck had gotten me closer in the crew. I spent most of the day hanging at Dom's and smoking weed. I didn't want to, but I saw no way of getting out of it. Turning down some of Dom's score would be like waving a narc flag over my head.

I hated how relaxed the drug made me feel. Like it took away the sharpness of my mind and dulled my thinking. How was I supposed to stay alert and listen to all their conversations to connect the dots if I was off in a weed-induced la-la land?

Not to mention it made me hungry as shit.

As soon as the sun went down and dusk claimed the sky, Dom told the crew to hit the streets to peddle his product. We were to hit up the regulars and try to bring in new clients.

I was paired with Tony, one of the crew. He was a young kid with brown hair and eyes. He seemed a little light in the brains department, but maybe that was just because he was high.

I said I would drive, hoping I was less stoned than he was, and we took off in the direction of where one of the regular buyers lived just a few blocks away. I stayed in the car as Tony made the deal. It was a fast exchange because Tony already had all the stuff the client wanted.

After that, we made a few more stops and then went to a nearby movie theater to hang out in the parking lot, where Tony said was a good place to find potential buyers. It totally pissed me off because movie theaters were places teenagers liked to hang out.

I made a mental note of every place we went so I could tell Watson to double up on the force's patrol in those areas.

We were sitting on the hood of the Mustang, smoking cigarettes (well, Tony was smoking; I was just pretending like I was going to light one up) when a movie let out and people began filing out the double doors of the theatre.

The last time I went to a movie was in Wilmington with Julie. My first date with her had been the best one I ever had. I missed her. I missed her laugh and her crazy hair. I wanted to feel her hips moving beneath me again and hear the hot little moans that escaped her throat when I did things— sexual things—to her body.

"Hey, kid," Tony said, pulling me out of my daydream. He was speaking to a passing teenager who looked to be about sixteen. He was following along right on the edge of his friends, looking the way I'd been feeling recently: on the outskirts of the group, looking in.

I had to hand it to Tony. He knew the ones to prey on.

The kid glanced up and Tony motioned for him to come over. "You in the market?"

"For what?" the kid asked, staring after his friends, who didn't even notice he stopped walking.

"For a good time," Tony replied.

"I don't do drugs," the kid said.

"That's cool," Tony said amicably. "You just struck me as the guy who likes to stand out in the crowd."

The kid stopped walking and turned back. "I am."

I stared at the kid, silently telling him to walk away and not get caught up in Tony's head games.

Tony nodded. "I figured. You seem like the life of the party, the one everyone else knows will show them a good time."

"You got something that'll be a good time?" the kid asked, his interest piqued.

"Yep. Me and my friend Gray here, we're the life of the party. Aren't we, Gray?" Tony looked at me for confirmation.

In that moment, I hated my job. And I hated myself for doing it. "You know it," I said, holding out my fist so he could pound it, which he did.

Tony glanced at the kid's friends, who were standing by a car and laughing. The blonde in the group slid a glance in our direction. "You ask her out yet?"

The kid's eyes widened. "She wouldn't go out with me."

"Sure she would!" Tony said. "All you gotta do is ask her. She keeps looking at you."

"She does?" he asked, looking at the girl.

Tony and I both nodded.

"I tried to ask her out once, but I got too nervous."

"Lucky for you I got something for that." Tony glanced around, then produced a small plastic sack of weed. "This here is called a confidence booster."

I thought about ripping the drugs out of Tony's hand and telling the kid to run. But I didn't.

"Take this, give it a smoke, and you and all your friends will be so chill that you won't even think twice about asking her out."

The kid reached out and took the sack. "How much is it?"

"It's free," Tony said. "Complimentary. Anything to help a bro out."

"Thanks," the kid said with a smile, slipping the drugs into the front pocket of his jeans.

"Anytime. I'll be here next weekend. Same time. You want more, bring some cash and I'll hook you up."

The kid agreed and then he jogged away, rejoining his friends.

Tony looked at me. "And that is how you reel in new clients."

"Let's get out of here," I said, feeling disgusted.

We made it out of the parking lot of the theater and were driving across the large, almost empty mall lot when a pair of familiar flashing lights appeared in my rearview mirror.

"We got company!" Tony yelled, panic in his voice.

"Maybe they just need by," I said, hopeful. The last thing I needed was some cop blowing my cover tonight.

I pulled out of their way and waited for them to drive by.

They didn't.

The officer pulled up behind me and put it in park.

As if this night hadn't been bad enough.

21

Julie

"Julie?" Susan said, bringing me out of my own head.

I blinked and glanced at her sharply. "Yes?"

"Would you mind closing up the salon when you're finished? I have an awful headache. I'd like to go home."

I offered her a smile. "Of course. It's been a long week."

Susan smiled wearily. "Yes, it has. But business is great so I can't complain."

I never thought of Susan as a fake person. Until now. It's like she acted and looked one way, but the words coming out of her mouth just didn't match. She always seemed a little uptight (or anal, as I liked to call her), and I just thought it was because of the responsibility of running a successful salon… Now I wondered if perhaps there was more to it.

"I'm just going to finish up in the back. Then I'll lock up for the night."

"Sounds wonderful. Feel free to use the phone on my desk to call the distributor."

"Great! Thanks so much. Have a great night!" I gave her a little wave and then went into the back room, sagging against the wall.

My thoughts went to Blue. I felt like I needed to tell him about what I heard. What I saw. I didn't have a way to contact him, though. Even if I did, what would I say? I could tell him all my suspicions. I could just relay what I knew and let him look into it.

My mind rejected that right away. He was already tired. He was already dealing with so much. It felt wrong to just dump all my uncertainties in his lap and expect him to figure it out.

What I needed was a plan.

I was good at plans.

Look how well my plan of a can of hairspray and a razor worked out. If that had been an actual burglar, I would have totally gotten away.

Evidence would be good too.

Something that he could use against Dom.

I picked up my cup of abandoned coffee and took a sip while I thought. My nose wrinkled and I looked down at the liquid. It was cold.

Ew.

Carrying the mug over to the microwave, I stuck it in and hit a few buttons, then stood waiting for it to heat up.

Dom said he wanted to see the product. Something told me he wasn't talking about hair product. He also said something about his business and Susan turning on him.

I knew from Blue that Dom's business was drugs.

It seemed almost asinine that Susan was involved in the drug business. It was the mention of another person that made me not completely reject the idea. She accused Dom of killing someone, someone who clearly meant a lot to her.

Maybe I wasn't the only person who got tipsy on a man. Maybe Susan was in love with someone who worked for Dom. Maybe that guy dragged her into his mess.

Wait.

Rewind that.

Did I just say *love?*

Yeah, I had been talking about Susan, but the implication was that she was like me. That I was like her.

I was confusing myself.

Point is I kind of implied that I was in love with Blue.

Was I?

In lust? Heck yes. Had feelings for him? Absolutely. In love? It was too soon for the L-word.

Right?

The microwave dinged and I welcomed the distraction. Thinking about my feelings for Blue wasn't going to help him with this case. I could think about that later.

I sipped the newly warmed coffee. Ahhhh. It was good.

So. *If* Susan was somehow involved with Dom and *if* he had come here to check up on his product… that product had to be drugs.

Susan was keeping drugs in this salon.

But where?

My eyes went directly to the door in the room. The room that supposedly held the water heater and electrical stuff.

But what if there was more?

I peeked back out into the salon at Susan's office. The light was off and the rest of the salon was empty.

It was a good time to be sneaky.

I went straight for the door and turned the handle, giving it a good yank.

It was locked.

Interesting.

"If I were a key, where would I be?" I asked myself, looking around the room for a spare key. I searched through all the drawers, looked under the sink, behind the fridge, and around the doorframe.

It was nowhere to be found.

I wasn't going to be deterred. I strode out to my station and dug around for a bobby pin. Hey, if MacGyver could build bombs with some duct tape and a tube of toothpaste, then I sure as hell could pick a lock with a bobby pin.

Using my teeth, I separated the little metal prongs and then slid the end into the lock. It took quite a few tries.

Okay, it took ten.

On the eleventh try, the handle turned and I smiled. Leaving the bobby pin sticking out of the handle, I pushed it open and went inside.

It was dark, but overhead was a bare bulb hanging from the ceiling. I yanked the little chain dangling down and the room flooded with light.

There was a water heater and circuit breaker box in here, along with some old brooms and dustpans and a vacuum from the nineteen fifties. But among those things were also boxes.

Boxes of hair color.

Why in the world would she have me order all that hair color when we had boxes of it sitting in here?

Suspicion tasted worse than cold coffee. Looking over my shoulder to make sure I was still alone, I crept closer to the boxes.

Pulling down one of the cardboard boxes from the top, I dropped it at my feet, wincing because it was heavier than I expected it to be. After a few minutes of no one rushing in to see what the loud noise was about (thankfully, I was still alone), I knelt down to pull off the thin layer of tape sealing the box.

Once the top was completely open, I looked inside.

And frowned.

There in neat and symmetrical rows were the black boxes I knew so well. It was just developer. Developer was the stuff we mixed with the actual hair color; it was the stuff that actually changed the hair. It put the blond in blond. The higher the developer, the more lift you got in the shade of your hair.

Still not understanding why there would be so much of this stuff back here, I broke open one of the boxes and pulled out the clear bag of white powder.

I knew right away what was going on.

This powder wasn't as thick, wasn't as heavy as the developer I used every single day. It was finer, a little lighter looking. It was like sugar compared to flour.

But this wasn't sugar.

And this wasn't the same kind of clear bag the developer came in from the supplier.

I wasn't a druggie. I never even experimented with drugs as a teenager (it was too scary). But I knew cocaine when I saw it.

I'd found my proof.

Proof I kinda hoped I wouldn't find. I mean, what girl wanted to find out that her boss was in bed with a bunch of nasty scumbag drug dealers?

Not me.

I stood up, still holding the bag of cocaine in my hands. I had to find a way to get word to Blue. I had to tell him what I found.

I turned to rush out of the back room.

I gasped, stopping in my tracks, as I stared down the barrel of a pistol.

The bag of coke dropped onto the floor with a smacking sound, and I put my hands up in the air.

The police officer on the other side of the gun looked like he wasn't afraid to shoot.

"Ma'am," he said, his tone hard and very impolite, "you're under arrest."

"Arrest!" I gasped, flinging my hands out in shock.

His arms jerked and the gun pointed at me with renewed force. "Hands up!" he yelled.

I put them up. I heard footsteps rushing in from the front of the salon.

"In here!" the officer yelled, not taking his eyes off me.

"There's been a mistake." I tried.

He looked at me with unveiled disgust dripping from his features. "No mistake. You're under the arrest for possession of an illegal substance."

He glanced at the boxes lining the walls and then back at me. "Lots of it."

Two more police officers flooded the tiny back room, all of them taking in the situation and then looking at me.

A pair of handcuffs appeared, and I felt my shoulders slump.

This was not at all how my plan was supposed to go.

22

Blue

"License and registration please," the cop said, shining his flashlight right in my face.

I dug around and produced the items he asked for. He didn't even look at them. "What are you doing out tonight?"

"We just came from seeing a movie." I lied.

"You have any illegal substances in this vehicle?"

"No."

I could feel Tony fidgeting in the passenger seat. I wanted to snap at him to control himself, that his anxious behavior only made us look guilty, but I couldn't say a word.

"You mind if I take a look around, then?" the officer asked, friendly-like. I squinted up at his face, trying to see if I knew him. But the light from the flashlight was so blinding that I couldn't make out his features.

I shielded my eyes from the light and said, "Actually, I do mind."

Tony gasped and I stifled an eye roll. Dumb kid probably didn't even realize that he didn't have to let the cops search his car unless they had a warrant.

The officer regarded me stonily. "I'm going to have to ask you to step out of the vehicle."

He wanted to see if I was sober. He wanted grounds to arrest me or search this car. The officer stepped back so I could open the door and get out. I glanced at Tony, who was sweating profusely.

"Chill, man," I whispered.

"Dude, we are so busted."

"No, we aren't. I can handle this. Just play it cool. Stop fidgeting."

He nodded.

Both of us climbed out of the car. The officer studied me and then asked me to perform a few basic tests. I passed with flying colors.

He seemed irritated by this and adjusted the cap on his head. "Stay here," he said and then walked to his cruiser to run my plates and ID. I wondered what he would think when he realized I was undercover.

I couldn't see what he was doing in the interior of his car because it was so dark, and I didn't want to stare. Tony and I stood there for a while, the brisk night air pulling at our clothes as we waited.

Eventually the officer got out of his cruiser and walked toward me. Gone was the stiffness in his body. I prayed he didn't say something that would give me away.

"You know you blew that stop sign back there?" he asked.

What? No, I hadn't. I wasn't a careless driver. "No," I said strangely.

"That's the reason I pulled you over."

I glanced over at Tony, who was frowning. "He didn't run no stop sign," the kid argued.

"You arguing with an officer of the law?" the man snapped and shined his light directly in Tony's face.

Tony threw up his hand and shook his head rapidly. "No."

The officer looked back at me, lowering the light. I recognized his face immediately, and I turned so my back was to Tony and gave the man a glare.

He didn't so much as blink. "I'm giving you a ticket for failing to stop at the stop sign," he said.

I gave him a WTF look. He ignored me and began writing on his pad. A few seconds later, he turned his ticket pad toward me and clicked on the blindingly bright light again.

I had the urge to knock it out of his hands.

But then he shone it on my ticket. Which wasn't a ticket at all.

It was a note.

"You see here that you have this amount of time to respond," the officer pointed to the paper like he was explaining something as I read his hastily scrawled note.

He continued to explain to me how the ticket worked, but I stopped listening because the writing made my blood run cold.

Julie was brought in on drug charges. Julie is asking for you.

Come if you can.

"Thanks for explaining," I said, still staring at the words.

The officer ripped the fake ticket off his pad and handed it to me. I had to take it or Tony would think it was weird.

"Stay out of trouble," he warned and then went back to his cruiser and drove away.

"You were awesome," Tony said, relief clear in his voice.

"Thanks," I said, hollow, thinking about Julie and what the hell was going on. How the hell did she get arrested on drug charges?

I wondered if she asked for me. I wondered if she was scared.

I needed to get rid of Tony so I could go to the station and see her for myself. I started the engine, all the while brainstorming ways to get rid of my partner for the night. A cell phone rang and I stiffened, thinking of my department cell strapped under the seat. What if it was someone trying to reach me about Julie? What if something was seriously wrong?

I fought the urge to reach beneath the seat, my knuckles turning white on the steering wheel.

"It's Dom," Tony said, holding up his cell. Then his forehead wrinkled. "Hey, you okay?"

I forced my body to relax. "Yeah. I'm okay. That cop just shook me up." I lied.

"Could have fooled me," he said and silenced the ringing of the phone. "Hey, boss. What's up?"

He listened a minute and began to talk. "We're near the mall. We got pulled over. Blue was awesome, handled the cop with ease!"

I wasn't sure if Tony singing my praises was going to help me or not, but in that moment, I didn't care. I just wanted to know how Julie was.

"Yeah! We even scored a new client!" Tony was saying. He reminded me of an overeager puppy trying to please his master.

He fell quiet and I breathed a silent thank you. I could pretend I was sick and wanted to go home. But someone could come by my house, and if I wasn't there…

I could pretend I had a booty call… but with who? I refused to bring Julie into this anymore and act like it was her.

"Yeah, no problem," Tony said and then hung up the phone.

"Dom wants us to come back."

Good. I could dump Tony and figure out a way to leave. Driving would give me some time to think of a plan. Maybe I could somehow get a message to Slater and he could give me an out.

When I pulled up to the curb at Dom's, Tony opened the door before I could cut the engine. "Dom said you didn't have to come in." His voice was wary.

"Is there a problem?" I asked, finally realizing there might be something going on.

"No, I don't think so. He just wanted to talk supply business with me." His eyes shifted away.

"Ahhh, crew business that I'm not allowed to be involved in."

Tony's face blanched. I could tell he felt bad. "Yeah. Look, I'm sure Dom will come around."

I held up my hand and cut him off. "It's cool, Tony."

"Really?" he asked, looking hopeful. If I hadn't just witnessed him giving drugs to a kid, I might actually like the guy.

"Yeah. I'll see ya later."

He slammed the door and it took everything in me to not peel away from the curb like a bat out of hell. After letting the engine idle for a few seconds, I pulled out onto the street at a normal speed. A few blocks over, I couldn't take it anymore and I pushed on the gas pedal and sped toward the station.

23

Julie

Interrogation rooms smelled. Well, I don't know about all of them, because this was the first one I ever had the dishonor of being kept in. But still, it smelled. The tiny square room was filled with stale air tinged with sweat and possibly urine. It made me very afraid about the chair I was sitting in and who may or may not have peed in it.

I thought for a long time about asking for a Lysol wipe.

I figured there was no use because I likely wouldn't get it. They wouldn't even take the handcuffs off my wrists.

Aside from the Lysol wipe, the only other thing I could think of was if I was going to have to mark that box on every application that I filled out from now on:

☒ Has been arrested for committing a felony.

Did that mean I would forever be considered a criminal? Or was that only if I was found guilty? Wait. Was this going to go to trial?

Clearly, I was not handling this well.

And I hadn't even been questioned yet. They literally stuffed me in the back of a squad car, drove to the station, and shut me in this interrogation room. They tried to ask me one question, and I demanded to speak to Blue.

Not a lawyer. Blue.

Except the minute I asked for Blue, a hush fell over the room and everyone left. I heard some yelling a while ago, but no one had been in since.

I wasn't sure if that was a good thing or a bad thing.

I kind of wished I hadn't drunk that coffee earlier. I kinda understood why my chair smelled like urine now.

I had to pee.

How long were they going to leave me in here? I felt like an animal chained up and shoved in a cage.

Holy moly… were they going to put me in a cell? That was like an *actual* cage.

It would serve them right if I peed right here and now!

Take that, idiots who arrest law-abiding citizens! Clean up my pee!

Yes. Clearly being incarcerated made me unstable and dramatic.

Whatever.

As more minutes wore on, some of my anger and frustration wore away and was just replaced by anxiety. I realized things looked really bad for me. I was literally caught with a huge stash of drugs, with some of them in my hand.

Yeah, I was going to try and tell them it was all a misunderstanding. I would tell them about the conversation I overheard, about how I went looking for stuff I really didn't expect to find.

Would they believe me?

I didn't know and frankly, I was kind of scared to talk. I was afraid I would just make things worse. I guessed I was going to have to get a lawyer. I would probably lose my job over this.

I wanted Blue.

If Blue were here, he could vouch for me. He would believe what I said. Maybe he would convince the other guys I wasn't lying. He could be like a character witness.

Only I didn't know where Blue was or where he lived. Hell, I didn't even know what kind of car he was driving. I wasn't sure if they would let him come to the station for this; it could compromise his cover.

The headache threatening me earlier decided to add to my torment by beginning to scream behind my eyes. My stomach felt nauseous and my hands and knees were shaking from all the stress I suddenly felt.

I closed my eyes against the harsh fluorescent light overhead and leaned forward, resting my overheated forehead on the table. It was cool and felt a little soothing against my headache.

I needed a plan.

A plan would make me feel better. More in control.

Whenever the officers came back, I would make them let me go pee. Then I would demand my one phone call. I would call Dee and she could post bail (would I need bail?) and get me out of here. I would get a lawyer, who'd probably charge all of my savings just to talk to me. But I would hire him anyway. I would rather be poor than in the big house with burly women named Wilma.

After that, I would let the police question me. I would tell my story. I would stick to the truth.

The truth would set me free.

Why did that sound like the most pathetic line ever?

I took a deep breath. It was a good plan.

I turned my head and rested my cheek on the brown tabletop and stared at the wall across the room. I wondered if someone was watching me through the two-way mirror behind me. If so, they were going to be very bored.

I heard the doorknob rattle, but I didn't bother to turn my head and look. I had no desire to see disgusted looks of the men who brought me in. Being treated like a criminal sucked. I guess that explained all the chase scenes in movies when the bad guys were running from the cops. Running was better than this.

The door flew open and all the air in the room shifted, like it was being sucked out with the force of the opening door. Fresh air from the station leaked in; it was much cooler and fresher smelling.

A string of expletives echoed around the room. Someone was good and pissed off.

I knew that voice.

I jerked upright, blinking against my headache at Blue, who was striding into the room.

"Blue," I said, relief so palpable in my tone that I could taste it in the back of my throat.

"What the fuck is this!" he roared, throwing out his hands and turning around to face whoever was standing in the doorway. "You *fucking* cuffed her!"

Another voice from out in the hall, a more calm and authoritative voice, said, "Give him the damn cuff keys." I heard the jangle of keys and saw Blue snatch them out of the air. Then behind him I heard the same voice mutter, "Idiots."

Blue was at my side in seconds, kneeling down so we were about eye level. "Hey there, sweetness."

I didn't say anything because all of a sudden I felt like crying. His gentle tone meant just for me was going to be my undoing.

I had missed him. Yeah, it hadn't been very long since our night together, but it seemed that the only time I ever got with Blue was stolen moments. Little pockets of time where he filled me up so completely but then left, leaving that fullness to drain away like a too-old battery.

Not only that, but worrying about his safety, where he was, who he was with. Not being able to talk to Dee or anyone about him. And then this… the drugs, the arrest.

He reached around behind me, looping his arms around my waist, and had the cuffs gone within seconds. My arms fell forward in my lap and my shoulders felt numb and prickly from being in the same position for so long.

Blue grabbed my wrists, rubbing them, like someone would do when they were out in the snow too long and needed to generate warmth.

"Rough night, huh?" he asked gently.

I nodded. "I have to pee."

He chuckled. "Come on." He stood, drawing me to my feet, and led me to the door. Two officers who had been at the salon stood in our path.

Blue angled himself in front of me. "Step aside," he said. His words weren't demanding or mean, but there was steel in them.

The men moved and we walked out of the tiny room. I breathed a sigh of relief. Blue walked beside me, glancing out of the corner of his eye.

"That room smelled like urine."

He made a face and looked over his shoulder. "You put her in Potty John's room?" he growled.

"It was the only room open!" one of the guys defended.

We stopped in front of a bare door to what I prayed was the ladies' room. "Who's Potty John?" I had to know.

Blue grinned. "One of the local drunks. He gets hauled in here all the time and the guys put him in one of the interrogation rooms to sleep it off." He cleared his throat. "He has a tendency to, uh… piss himself."

I laughed but quickly slapped a hand over my mouth. Nothing about this night was funny.

Blue got an angry look on his face and gestured to the door with his chin. "I'll wait here."

I nodded and rushed inside to quickly do my business. At the sink, I ran cold water from the tap and splashed it over my face after I washed my hands. Using a paper towel, I dried my skin and then wiped up the raccoon eyes my mascara had given me.

I felt bone tired. Not just bone tired, but weary. I knew it was the reason I felt so emotional, and damn, if looking at Blue wasn't making it worse.

I wanted to go home, but I knew it wasn't going to happen for a while.

After glancing at my less-than-stellar reflection in the mirror, I gave a sigh and trudged to the bathroom door. Before pulling the handle, I stood up and pulled my shoulders back. I might be exhausted and scared, but I wasn't going to show all the men out there that.

Blue wasn't in the doorway like I thought he would be. He was a few feet away. His back was turned and he was speaking to a few nearby men in uniforms. Judging from their expressions, he wasn't saying very nice things.

One of the officers who arrested me looked up, noting my reappearance. Blue stilled, said something, and the officers walked away. They didn't go far, though, stopping at the end of the hallway and watching me.

Like I was a criminal.

Something inside me snapped.

I glared at them. "Y'all are a bunch of idiots!" I spat. "You've done nothing but waste everyone's time tonight."

Blue was at my side instantly, wrapping a warm palm around my elbow. "Julie," he murmured.

I glanced at him, anger bubbling up inside me like a soda that was shaken up too much. "Don't." I growled. "Don't you dare tell me to shut up. That was nice compared to the things I'm thinking about them."

I swear his lips twitched. "I wasn't going to tell you to shut up. You can yell at them all you want."

"Thank you." I sniffed and resisted the urge to stick my tongue out at the men in the hall.

"Come on," he said, tugging me gently and leading me down the hall and past the officer's on my shit list.

"I am not going back in that room," I said, dragging my feet.

"That's not where we're going," he replied calmly. He led me into a private office with a desk and all the usual office furnishings. The most interesting thing in here was a half-dead plant. Once I cleared the threshold, Blue shut the door behind us.

"Are you going to interrogate me now?" I asked a little bitterly.

He didn't say anything, but I felt his penetrating sapphire stare. He took a step forward. Then another. He came so close that I could feel the heat off his body and smell the scent that seemed to be his calling card. His chest rose and fell evenly with his relaxed breathing. He was wearing the same leather jacket he wore the other night, and the gray knit cap was on his head.

I was ready for the barrage of questions. I was ready for him to ask for my statement.

I was less prepared for his arms.

He wrapped them around me, pulling me tightly against his chest. Basically wrapped himself around me, making me feel small. In that moment, if I would fit, I would have let him put me in his pocket.

I buried my nose in the soft fabric of his red T-shirt, wrapping my arms around his middle, beneath the leather of his coat. His palm came up to stroke the back of my head, and I felt the brush of his lips on the top of my head.

"I'm sorry." He murmured, rocking us both a little. The swaying motion was oddly comforting.

"What're you sorry for?"

"That it took me so long to get here."

"How'd you know I got arrested?"

"You asked for me, didn't you?"

I snorted against his chest. "Yeah. But after I asked for you, they pretty much left me in that pee-ridden room to rot."

He chuckled. "They knew they screwed up. Soon as they told Watson who they arrested, he contacted me."

I glanced up. "But how would he know who I was?"

He kissed my forehead. "Because I told him."

"You did?"

He nodded. "You matter."

It was a simple two words. They carried so much weight. I felt tears well up behind my eyes.

"You matter too," I whispered.

He smiled.

"I had a plan to help you."

He groaned, cutting me off. "Please tell me this isn't the result of one of your *plans*."

I nodded. "It was a good one." I paused. "Well, until the cops showed up."

He looked horrified. "What the hell kind of hare-brained *plan* are we talking about here?"

I released his waist and stepped back so I could meet his eyes full-on. "I know where the drugs are, and I know who's been helping Dom."

24

Blue

Being back at the station was slightly jarring. It was so familiar here, yet it seemed foreign. I spent so much time over the last several months undercover, I had barely been here at all. Just when I was getting back into things, they pulled me back undercover again.

Being here was almost like walking into the past, or having a strange sense of déjà vu. Of course, I couldn't really think about that because I was so focused on the reason I was here. Julie got herself arrested.

For drugs.

I would have laughed at the ridiculousness of it all if I wasn't imaging her here somewhere… scared. What the hell was going on? How the hell had this happened?

Fuck, if I hadn't called and told Watson about her, they might have ignored her request when she asked for me.

Please don't let this have to do with my case. The whole drive here, the thought replayed in my head over and over like a bad song on the radio. The thought of her caught up in any of this—with those drug-dealing lowlifes—made me want to put my fist through a wall.

As a cop, I knew what I would find when I walked into the station. Yet seeing her hunched over the table, with her hands freaking cuffed behind her back, was something I could never have been prepared for.

The rage that swept through my body was like a sudden tsunami, rising up out of the calm ocean and sweeping everything out of its path. I knew those men thought they were doing their job, but I wanted to beat them all to a pulp.

Couldn't they see what I saw?

Didn't they see the innocence behind her eyes, the honesty in her expression? How is it that anyone could look at her and think she was guilty of being involved with drugs that were killing kids?

Fucking idiots. All of them.

Yeah, okay, maybe I was being harsh. They were doing their job. They were trying to protect people. Looks could be deceiving… I kind of built my undercover identity on that, but I couldn't help how I felt. Even if it was biased.

Then she uttered the words I had been praying she wouldn't say. *I know where the drugs are, and I know who's been helping Dom.*

I tried to reign in my reaction until I had all the facts. It was a good exercise in self-control.

"Sit down," I told her after she dropped her bomb. "You look like you're about to pass out."

"It's been a long day," she murmured as she sat.

"You hungry? Want some coffee or something?"

She shook her head. "Maybe just some water."

They haven't even given her water? "How long you been here?" I asked, a little more harsh than I intended.

She shrugged. "I really don't know."

I yanked open the office door. "I need some bottled water in here," I barked.

Watson appeared in the doorway, giving me a measured look. "You getting comfortable in my office?"

I had to admit this crappy, depressing office was a lot better than my tiny house in the ghetto. "No, sir. Didn't mean to take over. I just wanted somewhere private to talk to her."

Watson nodded and stepped into the room. "Julie Preston I presume," he said, stopping before her chair and looking down.

Julie straightened her shoulders and lifted her chin to meet his gaze. "Yes, sir," she said and offered her hand to give him a solid handshake.

Watson looked impressed.

"I do apologize for the way you were treated. The arresting officers are young and eager."

"It's fine," she said coolly.

"I admit, it doesn't look good—the way you were found, I mean." He continued.

"I wasn't aware people were looking for me. A simple phone call and I would have come in on request."

I smothered my smile as Julie held her own with my boss. One of the secretaries out front appeared with several bottles of chilled water, and I gave her a wink as I took them and shut the door to the office.

"We weren't looking for you specifically," Watson said, glancing at me.

I twisted off the cap to a water and handed it to Julie. She took a small sip. "Right before you came in, she said she knew where the drugs were coming from and who was helping Dom."

Watson sat forward with an eager look in his eyes. "Tell us."

She opened her mouth to explain, but I stepped in front of her, silencing her words. "She's getting immunity for this, right?"

Watson sighed.

"The charges will be dropped. Her name will be kept out of the case," I said.

"I think we can work that out." Watson agreed. "Her name will be in the police files. Her statement will be in there too of course, but we can keep her out of the press."

Satisfied, I yanked a chair with metal legs over near Julie and sat down beside her. "You can talk now," I told her.

She rolled her eyes. "Thanks for the permission."

I ignored her smartass tone. "You're welcome."

Watson watched us with veiled amusement. I would likely hear about this later.

"Can I ask a question first?" Julie asked, directing her words at Watson.

He nodded.

"Why were the police at the salon tonight?"

He cleared his throat. "We had an anonymous tip."

"A tip about what?"

"Drugs," he said simply.

Annoyance flashed through me. "Why wasn't I notified? This is my case."

"Because you're undercover. You would have been notified after we verified the tip," Watson replied.

"Do you know if it was a man or woman that called in the tip?"

He glanced down at a stack of papers on his desk. "A female."

"She set me up," Julie murmured, sounding shell-shocked.

"What?" I asked.

Julie was quiet a moment as she worked through whatever it was in her mind. Then she looked up. "The owner of the salon, Susan Highland, is probably the one who called in the tip. She was the only one who knew I was there tonight. She knew I was alone. She asked me to lock up."

"Why would she do that?" I asked.

"Because she's the one who's been working with Dom. She's the one who's been holding the drugs."

"Explain how you know this, Miss Prescott." Watson urged.

"Several weeks ago, my boss Susan asked me if I would take on more responsibility at the salon. She wanted me to start doing the inventory—you know, keeping track of our hair supplies, our products, things like that."

Watson and I both nodded so she continued.

"She also asked me to take over the display and things. I thought it was a little strange that she wouldn't ask someone more senior, but she said it was because I had the youthful vibe she wanted to represent the salon." Julie sounded disgusted. "Now I know that it was because she just thought I would be gullible enough to take the blame."

"How does any of this connect with the drugs and this case?" Watson asked impatiently.

"I heard her on the phone recently, after hours, arguing with someone. Saying there wasn't enough room for something. It was an awkward conversation, and when she was done, she seemed flustered and upset. I didn't really think much about it until what happened earlier."

"What happened?" I asked.

"I had to stay late to finish the inventory so I didn't have to go in tomorrow. I was the last one left. I was in the back room, out of sight. Susan was in her office. Someone came in the salon and I overheard him and Susan arguing." She glanced at me sheepishly. "I listened at the door."

I nodded.

"The guy seemed a little familiar, but I didn't realize who it was at first. Anyway, he was demanding to see the 'supply,' and I was going to hide, but then I heard him slap her." She paused for a moment and took a sip of water. I couldn't help but notice how her hand trembled finely. "I went out into the salon. It was Dom."

"You're sure it was him?" Watson asked.

"I'm sure. I met him before. I think he might have recognized me."

"Then what happened?" I didn't like where this was going.

"Dom left. Susan seemed upset and she asked me to close up. After she left, I got curious… I knew you were looking for the drugs, and after hearing Susan and Dom, I suspected they were at the salon."

"You went looking for them?" I groaned. "You should have called me."

"I don't have your number," she snapped.

"So you found them and that's when my officers arrived, finding you with a room full of drugs."

Julie nodded at Watson, relieved that he understood. "Yes, exactly. I swear those drugs aren't mine. I found them. Really!"

"We believe you," I assured her, slipping my arm around her shoulders.

"How does a salon owner fall into business with a drug cartel?" Watson asked in a thoughtful tone.

Julie perked up. "She mentioned something to Dom about a guy. She accused Dom of killing him. She said that Dom was lying to her, keeping her on a string so she would keep working for him."

"Milo." I swore.

Watson and Julie both turned to me.

I glanced at Watson. "It's why Slater is undercover, the cop from Raleigh. They suspect that Dom killed one of his men, a guy named Milo. This could be the break they need," I murmured.

"So," Watson surmised. "You think Susan Highland got roped into the drug business by her boyfriend/lover and then Dom killed him?"

Julie nodded enthusiastically. "Yes, but Dom told her that Milo was out of town so she would keep hiding the drugs. They were all disguised in boxes of hair color and developer. No one would have suspected unless they were a hairstylist."

I cussed. It was the fucking perfect set-up.

"You believe me… right?" Julie asked, unsure.

"Yes, sweetness. We believe you." I lightly massaged the back of her neck with my hand.

"Sweetness?" Watson said, arching his brow.

Julie laughed. I pretended like I hadn't heard.

"We'll need to bring in Ms. Highland for questioning. Hopefully she'll roll over on Dom."

Julie sat up. "She will. Especially thinking that he killed Milo. She was getting choked up just talking about him. I actually feel kind of bad for her."

"Don't," I said, harsh. "She deserves to be punished. There's no excuse for what she's been doing. People have died."

Julie paled and I wanted to kick myself. She already looked awful, with dark circles beneath her eyes.

"This is exactly what we needed," Watson said, gleeful.

"What's going to happen now?" Julie asked, not nearly as thrilled as my boss.

Adrenaline began to pump through my system like water through a hose. "Now I'm going to break this case wide open."

25

Julie

All the charges against me were dropped. Well, technically I don't think they actually charged me with anything to begin with, but whatever.

Blue thought my plans were hare-brained. Shows how much he knew. My plan broke the case. Hopefully now they could do whatever they were going to do and be done with it.

Blue wouldn't tell me anything after I spilled everything I knew. One look at Watson told me I wouldn't get any help there either. Basically as soon as they got all the info they needed, I was ushered out of the room to sign some papers and stuff while Blue stayed in the office, no doubt hatching some "official police business" plan.

Men.

O_o ← that's me rolling my eyes.

Not too much later, Blue appeared and motioned for me to join him back in the office while Watson went off in another direction.

"Hey," he said, shutting the door and pushing me up against it. His body pressed into mine. The weight felt delicious, and suddenly I didn't feel quite as exhausted as before.

"Hey, yourself."

He dipped his head, capturing my lips and pulling them into a tangled-up kiss. I melted against the door as our lips intertwined deliciously. My fingers found their way beneath the hem of his shirt, and I scraped my nails across his lower back, bringing him even closer. The hardness between his legs was unmistakable as he ground his hips against me.

A small sound of appreciation ripped from my throat and he yanked his mouth away, breathing heavy. "Damn," he said, breathless. "You make me forget this is my boss' office."

I lifted a brow. "What if it was your office?"

He smiled mischievously. "If it was my office, you'd already be lying across that desk with half your clothes off."

"So is this all I gotta do to see you more often? Get arrested?"

He growled and scooped me up in his arms. My head fell back so I could look up at him. "Don't even think about making this a habit."

"This definitely will not be my new hobby." I assured him.

He pressed his forehead against mine and groaned. My insides quivered at his nearness. "I gotta go."

Disappointment stole away the giddy feeling of the moment. "Is being here going to cause trouble for you?"

"Nah. Don't worry about me. I'll be fine."

"What's going to happen?" I asked. I couldn't stop the fear that coiled through me. It was like an oversized snake, wrapping around and squeezing until my bones began to feel the pressure.

He planted a soft, full kiss on my lips before pulling away completely. I pressed my lips together, trying to hold on to him just a little bit longer.

"You're going to call Dee. You're going to tell her you were arrested and you need a ride."

That was *so* not going to happen. I shook my head. "Nuh-uh."

He crossed his arms over his chest. "Leave through the front of the building with her. Have her drive you home. There will be an unmarked officer behind you. He's going to be staked out by your place all night."

"What!" I shrieked, except it wasn't really a shriek because I was so tired my voice had turned hoarse.

"Dom saw you. He already has you connected with me." He ran a hand over his head, sliding the cap back so a few wayward dark-blond strands stuck out of the front, falling over his forehead. "Fuck. I didn't want you involved in this. I can't be with you tonight, but I'm going to make sure you're safe."

"Where will you be?" I asked, rubbing my arms against the sudden chill I felt.

"Working."

"I wish you were some grocery bagger at the supermarket," I muttered.

He laughed, but then he turned sober. "I wouldn't blame you if you decided this was too much. That *I* was too much."

"I haven't seen near enough of you to have my fill yet."

"So what's your limit? How big of an appetite do you have?" he asked, arching a brow.

Our conversation was playful, but underneath, I knew what he was really asking. I knew what he wanted to know but wasn't so sure how to ask. It made me wonder how many women had gotten a taste of life with a cop and ran the other way.

"I'm not going anywhere, Blue," I whispered. "It seems when it comes to you, I don't have a limit."

"Is that so?" Heat penetrated his eyes.

I nodded. "You've never called, you stood me up, you 'broke' into my house, and you're hardly ever around…" He frowned at his impressive list of flaws. "But I can't quit you."

"You strapped a pink cape around my neck, come up with the most ridiculous plans I've ever heard, have managed to drag yourself into a drug war, but I can't quit you either."

I smiled and wrapped my arms around his waist, pressing my cheek against his chest. "Think we'll change our minds when we have more time together?"

"No."

I didn't think so either.

I enjoyed the feel of him against me before I got back to the matter at hand. "My car is still at the salon."

"Leave it. Someone can take you over there tomorrow in broad daylight to get it." When I didn't argue, he said, "You have keys to the salon?"

"Yes."

"Can I have them?"

"They're in my bag. In that room." I was going to have to throw away that perfectly nice handbag. It spent too much time in Potty John's room to ever be usable again."

"Call Dee," he said, pulling me back, placing his hands on my shoulders and looking directly into my eyes. "Go home. Lock your doors. Officer Sander will be outside. You might not see him, but he'll be there."

"Do you think something will happen?" I couldn't help but worry.

"Dom would have to have a death wish to come after you." He growled. "But I sure as hell won't send you home without any kind of protection."

"When will I see you again?" All this doom-and-gloom talk was making me anxious.

"Soon."

Vague answers were stupid. Because they were vague. I liked definitive answers. I liked to know how many hours I was going to have to worry and wonder about him.

"Lay low, okay?" he asked, taking my hand and intertwining our fingers.

"I don't think that's going to be a problem considering I'm pretty sure my boss trying to frame me for drug trafficking was a quirky way of saying you're fired."

"I'm sorry, Jules."

I loved that he called me Jules. Yeah, it was only my name shortened, but it spoke of familiarity, of comfort. It was something a friend or someone close to me would use.

"Guess I better call Dee. She's gonna flip."

"Don't tell her too much."

"I won't."

He released my hand and walked toward the door.

He stopped.

He turned.

He swept me up into his arms and crushed our mouths together. Even though there was urgency surrounding us, urgency in the way we kissed, Blue still took his time. The way our tongues lingered against one another left me slightly dizzy.

"I'll see ya later, sweetness," Blue said when he pulled away.

"Bye," I whispered, practically melting into a nearby chair as he vacated the room, pulling the door around as he went.

I sat there a while, pretty much in a daze. Until reality set in and I realized I was free to go. Hanging around here any longer was not my idea of a good time. I picked up the phone on the desk and dialed Dee.

After several long rings, she picked up, with a sleep-filled voice. "This better be good."

"Dee? It's me. Listen, I got arrested. I need you to come pick me up at the police station in Jacksonville."

"Is this a prank call?" she asked, much more alert but now totally suspicious.

"I sorta wish it was."

"This better not be about *him*," she spat.

I sighed. "Are you coming or not?"

"Of course I'm coming," she bickered. "But I'm wearing my pajamas."

"See you in a few," I said and hung up.

The door to the office opened and Watson entered the room. He was carrying my bag, which he extended to me.

"Thank you," I said, taking it and looking through it to make sure all my belongings were there. I couldn't help but wrinkle my nose at the faint smell of urine. "You really need to Lysol that room," I told Watson.

He grunted. "I just consider it extra punishment for the criminals."

"Well, isn't that police work at its finest?" I quipped.

He cracked a smile. "Did you call for a ride?"

"Yes, she should be here soon. I'll just wait out front."

"Stay in the building until she pulls up."

I nodded and a small sliver of fear snaked its way up my spine. Would Dom come after me for this? Would he even know I was arrested? Would he think I had something to do with his stash being busted? How safe was I?

"Do you think he knows I got arrested?"

Watson regarded me seriously; his brown eyes were kind. "I honestly can't say. It's possible, but then again, he might not know. I should know more when they bring in Susan for questioning first thing in the morning."

Well, that didn't really make me feel better.

"I have a patrolman assigned to sit outside your house in an unmarked vehicle. He will watch your house overnight. Keep your doors locked and you'll be fine. If you have any problems, scream loudly or flick the lights and he'll come inside."

"Thank you."

"No, thank you. This is the information we've been looking for. This very well could be the break in the case that we needed. You've saved a lot of lives by coming forward tonight."

"I didn't exactly come forward," I said, annoyed. "I was arrested."

"Yes. Well. My apologies."

I sighed. "No need to apologize. Those men were doing their job."

Watson sat down behind his desk. I felt a little pang of sorrow for him. He looked exhausted. This case seemed to be wearing on everyone.

"Well, I'll just go wait out there. Good luck with the case."

"Blue called me about you," he said, stopping my progress out the door.

I turned back. "He told me."

"First time he's ever asked for anything, and it wasn't even for himself."

"He asked you for something?"

Watson didn't seem surprised that I didn't know that. "Asked me to watch out for you. I get the impression you're very important to him."

I felt a pang in my chest; a homesick feeling unfurled in my belly and filled me with longing. Yeah, I just saw Blue, but I desperately wanted to see him again. "He's very important to me as well," I replied softly before turning around and leaving the office.

26

Blue

The Mustang I was driving was parked quite a distance from the station, on a back street that didn't get much traffic. I let it sit there and headed out to the impound lot.

I needed an undercover vehicle that was more undercover than my undercover car.

So I borrowed a pickup truck. It was an old Ford with peeling red paint that had been sitting on the lot for over six months. I'm surprised cobwebs didn't fly out of the tailpipe when I turned on the engine.

But it would suit what I needed it for, no problem, and there was the added bonus that it looked like some old man's truck so it shouldn't attract too much unwanted attention.

I turned out of the lot and headed in the opposite direction from which I was actually heading. I could hear an internal ticking clock, reminding me that I didn't have much time, but being discreet was very important.

I circled around the town for a while, keeping an eye on my rearview mirror, watching the traffic and being sure that I wasn't being followed. I knew the possibility was slim, but I wasn't going to leave anything to chance.

Finally I turned onto the street of Razor's Edge Salon. I pulled into the parking lot quickly and drove around behind the building so from the street it appeared no one was there.

Julie's car was still sitting in the lot and my stomach tightened thinking about how close to this mess she was. All the more reason to get this case closed.

I let myself into the salon using the keys and crept through the darkness quietly. I paused, listening for the telltale signs that anyone else was in here. The place was still and quiet, and after several long moments, I did a quick sweep of the place just to be sure.

Once I was certain it was all clear, I went into the back room and moved into the open door of the storage room. Inside, I clicked on the single bulb overhead (there were no windows in here for the light to be seen at the street) and whistled between my teeth as I took in the boxes of drugs stacked all around, pretending to be innocent.

A little moment of satisfaction rippled through me because I had gotten here first. It seems the boys in blue at the station managed to keep Julie's arrest under wraps after all. Thank God.

The fact that I was here doing this wasn't really protocol for this situation and this amount of drugs, but it was necessary for closing this case. Seizing the drugs and splashing this all over the media would slow down the crew's operations, but it wouldn't stop them. Dom wouldn't pay for everything he'd done. The crew in Myrtle Beach wouldn't pay for the things they'd done either.

I didn't just want these drugs off the streets. I wanted the bastard scum who brought the drugs on the streets gone too. The fact that Watson agreed to this (and bending the rules) proved to me how badly he wanted the same things I did.

I hefted several of the boxes into my arms and made my way out to the truck. It took quite a few trips, but I moved quickly and managed to get all the drugs stacked into the bed of the old truck. I filled the entire bottom up with short stacks so no one would even know there was anything back there unless they physically approached the truck and looked.

After making sure the salon was the way I found it, I pulled out of the lot and didn't look back. Not too long later, my cell phone went off. I glanced at the screen and noted who was calling.

Show time.

"Dom," I answered. "What's up?"

"What are you doing right now?" he asked.

"Cruising the streets."

"It's time to move the shipment. Get here so I can take you to the stuff."

I agreed and then hung up. I couldn't help but wonder about the timing of this. Yeah, I'd been on standby for days now for the call to deliver the drugs. But the cop in me wondered if it wasn't a coincidence. Did he know the cops found the stash? Did the owner of the salon call him and brag she'd turned him in?

No. That would just be stupid. Susan Highland might be in bed with drug dealers, but she wasn't stupid. Hell, if she'd set up anyone besides Julie to take the fall for those drugs, it probably would have worked without an issue.

But she did set up Julie.

And Julie was more involved in this than people realized.

It didn't matter anyway. It didn't matter if Dom suspected anything because this was my shot, my clear shot at getting these guys. I was going in. I'd keep my eyes open, but I wasn't backing down.

I drove to the back street where the Mustang was parked. After sitting in a vacant lot across the street and watching the traffic (or lack thereof) and making certain there was no suspicious activity near my car, I steered the truck to the very end of the street and parked it beneath a broken streetlight.

I decided not to carry the Ford's keys with me. It would seem odd if someone in the crew saw me with more than one set of car keys. Instead of jamming them on my person or stashing them in the glove compartment of my car, I reached up under the wheel well of the back tire and found a small area to place the keys.

Yeah, it was crazy.

Crazy enough to work.

I mean, who in their right mind would leave the keys to a truck secretly stashed with millions of dollars worth of drugs in the back?

Me.

Without a backward glance, I drove away, heading straight for Dom's place.

His house had an attached one-car garage that was on the side of the house. When I pulled in, I noticed the garage door was open so I figured I'd just go in that way.

A few steps up to the garage and I realized my mistake.

My muscles tensed as my brain registered I wasn't alone.

The first hit came out of the darkness. His fist slammed into the back of my head, sending me stumbling forward into another punch that knocked my head back on my shoulders. Pain radiated from one side of my head to the other as I stumbled to catch my balance.

Three guys stepped out of the darkness, forming a triangle around me, closing in. Three against one. They weren't great odds. But I was pissed. I was tired and a fight didn't sound like a half-bad idea.

Shaking off the pain as best I could, my feet planted solidly on the concrete floor of the garage and I reached out, grabbing the front of a man's shirt with a great yank. I pulled him off balance and sent him flying into the bumper of the car parked in the garage. The man hit and I saw his back bow against the metal frame. He made a groaning sound as one of the others punched me in the jaw.

I struck out, my fist connecting with his gut, and he doubled over and I brought my knee up into his face. The sound of crunching bone gave me satisfaction. Using my leg, I swept out the broken man's feet and he fell back on the ground.

Preparing to knock him out completely, I yanked my arm back to throw down a punch, but someone caught it and spun me from behind.

The darkness swayed a little as I spun, and my stomach lurched. I caught another fist to the ribs and all my breath whooshed out of my body. Pain lanced through my chest and I bent over at the waist, fighting the urge to hurl.

Arms caught me from behind, linking through my biceps and twisting my arms back so I was rendered useless. The second man approached, and I kicked him. The kick didn't keep him down and he came back to deliver a series of blows that caused blackness to swim before my eyes.

I felt the warm ooze of blood as it trickled down my face, tracking a single line over my cheekbone like a tear. I twisted, catching the guy pinning me off guard, and fell to the side out of his embrace. I hit the floor, my knees taking the brunt of the fall, but I pushed up, not allowing myself to feel the sting of pain.

I grabbed the guy looming behind me and slammed his face into the side window of Dom's car. The glass didn't break, but the guy crumpled to a heap on the floor.

I squared off, facing the two remaining men. I knew they were both hurting, but so was I. This wasn't a fight I was going to win. We started at each other, throwing fists, taking hits, and I felt my skin swell as blood gushed from cuts on my face.

Several minutes later, the overhead light clicked on and the three of us drew back, blinking as our eyes adjusted to the new harsh lighting.

The sound of footsteps behind me caused my feet to move quickly, twirling my body around to see who was there.

It was Dom. "Maybe I should have sent more than three guys out here."

"Do I not looked fucked up enough for you?" I asked, squinting through the dripping blood and swelling facial features.

"You're still standing," he said, flat.

"It's gonna take a hell of a lot more than three guys to put me down and keep me there."

"I saw something today that was very unsettling," he said, ignoring my remarks.

I swiped at the mess on my face. "You look in the mirror?"

He lunged, snapping out his arm, connecting with my face, and then composing himself like he hadn't moved at all.

The insult was worth it. He disgusted me so much that I knew if I was packing heat, I would already be holding him at gunpoint.

"You should have told me the hot little piece you like to keep to yourself worked for one of my employees."

"What hot little piece are you referring to?"

"The one you so kindly let me know was off-limits."

I wiped at the blood on my lip. "You telling me you keep a hair stylist on your payroll? Do you not like making appointments like everyone else?" I snapped.

"You want the beating to continue?" he threatened.

"If you wanted me unconscious, I already would be."

He stared at me for long moments. Finally, the silence broke. "I want an explanation."

"Am I supposed to know what the hell you're talking about?" I crossed my arms over my chest and glared at him.

"Don't play stupid with me!" Dom yelled, some of his composure slipping a bit. "What are you, some kind of narc?"

I stiffened, like the term offended me. Then I lunged at him, hammering my ready fist into the side of his jaw. "I'm no narc!" I yelled.

"You might not be a narc," he said, dabbing at the corner of his busted lip, "but you are a traitor."

"How do you figure?"

"You trying to cozy up? Ingratiate yourself to me and the crew so you can edge me out and take over my neighborhood?"

"You invited me into the crew. I didn't come looking for you." I reminded him.

"Doesn't mean you won't take an opportunity when one is presented."

I didn't reply because he was right.

"So what? You have your bitch spying on me? On my business?"

My back teeth came together when he spoke of Julie like that. My body was stiff and sore, my face burned, and I was getting really, really cranky.

"I don't have time for this," I spat. "I did what you asked. I stole you a transport vehicle. I agreed to make the delivery. I went out on the street to deal. You even got my credits from LeBraun himself, and that ain't good enough."

I shook my head.

"Fuck this shit. I'm out." I turned to walk away.

"You're not out 'til I say you're out," he said quietly from behind.

The two men jumped me again and forced me to my knees. Anger burned through my veins, so hot and so putrid I wondered if perhaps it would burn holes right through my skin.

The door to the house opened and Slater came out behind Dom. He assessed the situation quickly, barely giving me a second glance. Before I knew what he was doing, he strode across the room, around Dom, and belted me in the face.

It was a low blow considering I was being forced down by two men already.

"What was that for?" I spat.

"For messing with Dom."

Dom clapped Slater on the back and stepped forward. He shoved his face close to mine, so close that I could smell the warm beer on his breath. "Do you know what happened to the last guy who tried to edge me out?"

I knew Slater was listening carefully.

"Why don't you tell me?" I invited.

"He also tried to use his woman to screw me out of millions of dollars." I stayed silent, looking straight into his eyes. "So I killed him."

Slater slipped, his body going completely rigid as the news—the confession—he'd been waiting for all this time was handed to him. Dom must have noticed the change in him and began to turn, but I couldn't let that happen.

"How do I know you aren't just bluffing?"

Dom swung back around, pinning me with a cold stare. It was the first time I saw the lack of conscience in his eyes. "You'll know for sure once I kill you and dump your body where I dumped his."

"I'm flattered you took the time to plan my burial."

Dom grunted. "No plan. Just taking out the trash."

I didn't dare look at Slater, but I hoped he got the message. Dom dumped Milo's body at one of the local trash yards.

From somewhere on his person, Dom pulled out a black Glock. It didn't appear so threatening, but I knew that one well-placed shot would end my life here and now.

I thought about Julie. About how my last moments with her would be at the police station, where she was dragged because of her involvement with me. I wanted to make it up to her… but now I wouldn't get the chance.

The gun leveled at me.

Then I remembered.

"Go ahead." I challenged. "Kill me. You'll never see your shipment again."

The gun jerked in Dom's hand. "What did you say?"

"I said I've got your drugs. All of them. You ever want to see them and your millions, you better not pull that trigger."

I could see him measuring my words. Weighing them against truth and bluff.

"Pretty genius idea disguising them as women's hair color and stashing them at a local salon. It's the last place anyone would think of."

His nostrils flared when he realized I really wasn't bluffing. A series of foul language dripped from his lips.

I smiled.

A phone started ringing. Dom lowered the gun, still keeping his eyes keen on my face, and answered his phone. "What?" he demanded.

His eyes turned cold and a calculating glint came across his features. I didn't like that look. I didn't like the calmness that came over him.

"Wait for my word," he instructed and then disconnected the call. "It appears we both have something the other wants."

"You ain't got nothing I want," I spat, my shoulders burning from being held down.

"Oh, I think you do. My men say she fought like a little hellcat and screamed until she was hoarse."

Julie.

Cold fury washed over my body. My reaction was so physical that I surged to my feet. Not even the two men holding me could keep me down. "What the hell have you done?" I spat.

"It seems I found your weakness and my bargaining chip to get back what belongs to me."

27

Julie

Dee and Craig pulled up in his black Hummer just a few minutes after I left Watson's office. The tail lights glowed in the dark as I pushed open the glass doors of the station and trudged wearily toward the curb.

The passenger-side window rolled down to reveal my best friend in all her pajama glory. They were blue with white clouds all over them. Her hair was pulled back in a messy bun and her eyes were alert.

"I've officially seen everything there is to see in life," she announced. "The least likely person on earth to be arrested has gone and been arrested. It's a sure sign the apocalypse is coming. Craig, better swing by Sam's Club on the way home so we can stock up on beans and SPAM."

"That's disgusting," I said as I climbed into the back seat. The interior of the Hummer was warm, and I sank into the black leather seat. "Remind me to never come to your house when zombie's take over America."

"That was me being hospitable-like. Beans are vegetarian."

I smiled as Craig pulled away from the curb and out onto the empty street. Dee peaked around her seat at me. "What the hell happened?"

I groaned. "It's a long story. I'm too tired to explain it."

"You think you can call me in the middle of the night to pick your ass up from the slammer and then not tell me why you got arrested in the first place?" she asked incredulously. She made a sound in the back of her throat. "I don't think so."

"Basically it was all a huge misunderstanding. They dropped the charges."

"What were the charges?" Craig asked.

"I can't really say. It's an ongoing investigation." Oh, that was good. *Good job, Julie*, I told myself for coming up with such an official response.

"Does this have anything to do with Blue?" Dee asked. She was like a dog with a bone. She wasn't going to give up.

"No." I lied.

I didn't really want to lie, but I had to. The less Dee knew the better. I didn't want her getting dragged into this. Not to mention, I really was told not to discuss this with anyone. I wasn't about to open my mouth and mess something up for someone. Blue was out there right now and the thought of him getting hurt literally made me feel like someone was ramming nails into my eyes.

Yeah, that was a gruesome image... I'd had a long night.

"I don't believe you," Dee said.

"You really should become a private investigator," I muttered.

"I knew it!" she burst. "You're such a lousy liar."

"I have no idea what you're talking about." I lied again, this time around a yawn.

"Uh-huh," she intoned. "You can tell me now or you can tell me in the morning when I show up at your front door."

I was saved from telling more lies she would never believe when Craig changed the subject as he gazed off to the side of the road. "Not a good time of night to be out on the road by herself," he muttered.

I looked around the seat and out the windshield at a car parked on the side of the road with the hood up and smoke rolling out from beneath. Leaning against the car was a woman wearing a pair of jeans and a too-large hoodie. She had long dark hair and a small build.

Craig slowed the Hummer and pulled several yards behind her car. "I'm just going to make sure she has a phone to call for help."

The woman looked at the Hummer warily, no doubt scared of who might be inside. If I were her, I wouldn't even have gotten out of my car. I would have locked the doors and called for help. But maybe Craig was right; maybe she didn't have a phone. Leaving her out here at this time of night wasn't right.

"I'll go with you," Dee offered. "Maybe seeing a woman will quell her thinking you're some kind of sicko who preys on women."

"I do not look like a sicko," Craig defended, and I laughed.

"That's the point," Dee said. "Most sickos look like normal guys."

"I'm not your average-looking guy," he grumbled as they opened their doors. "I'm extremely good-looking."

Dee snorted as she peeked at me in the backseat.

"I'll wait here," I said, not even having to feign exhaustion. The minute I got home, I was collapsing on the couch. I wasn't even going upstairs. I found that since my night with Blue, I preferred sitting in the living room. It made me feel closer to him.

"We'll be right back," she said and shut the door, joining Craig in front of the Hummer.

I leaned my head back against the seat and let out an exhale. I wondered what Blue was doing and hoped he was safe. I knew he was going to go after those drugs. He wouldn't tell me what he planned, but I knew he was planning something. It made me nervous. I always knew that dating a cop would be worrisome, but I never quite realized how much.

Dating? Why had my brain automatically gone there? We'd never so much as discussed our relationship, or lack thereof.

Lights shining through the back window had me lifting my head and looking to see who was there. Another car, some kind of truck, had pulled up behind us. Unease was like an icy finger against my skin, and I told myself to calm down. It was likely just another concerned driver stopping to see if any of us needed help.

I looked toward Craig and Dee. Craig was handing the woman his cell phone and the three were standing close together, talking.

I heard the slam of a door from behind and I waited for someone to pass by the Hummer on the way to talk to the small group of people standing outside.

But no one passed by and I swear it seemed like the headlights shining through the back window grew brighter… like they were getting closer.

I pivoted in the seat to look, and sure enough, the truck had driven up so that it was mere inches behind the Hummer.

"What the hell?" I muttered as the door next to me was yanked open forcefully.

I jerked as adrenaline flooded my body and a man with a dark hat and clothing reached into the vehicle to grab me. I slapped his arm away, sliding across the seat so he couldn't reach me. The man grabbed at my ankle and pulled me back, and I let out a scream, kicking at his face.

My boot connected with his jaw and he let out a deep grunt.

From outside, I heard Dee call my name and then a sharp cry. *Dee!* The man grabbed me by the arm and dragged me out of the car, and I let him, trying to see what was happening to my friends.

I fell out of the car and onto the ground, my knees taking the brunt of the fall. The man who was trying to attack me laughed and shoved me a little harder so I practically face-planted onto the pavement. "You deserve that, bitch," he said.

I pushed up, looking toward Craig and Dee. They were both standing with their hands in the air while the unassuming woman and a man were holding them at gunpoint.

Oh my God, were we being robbed?

Really? Like this day hadn't been shitty enough.

I sprang up and swung around to face the man who pulled me out of the car. I swung my fist at him and he dodged the hit. So I kicked him in the shin. When in doubt, just kick people.

"Shit," he swore when my boot connected with his leg.

I took off running, not really sure which way to go, but knowing I couldn't stay here. I was the only one that didn't have a gun pointed at my head so that meant I was the only one that could try to get help.

The sound of a gun discharging was like a deafening roar in my head. The bullet hit the pavement right next to me and little bits of gravel and earth flew up and hit my legs.

I screamed and automatically threw my hands up to protect my face, trying to come up with a plan. I should get in the Hummer and run them all down.

They could shoot at me all they wanted, but it was a big car and it would be moving.

"She's supposed to be alive," someone yelled, and awful awareness crashed over me. We weren't being robbed.

This was a kidnapping. Dom sent people after me. I put my friends in grave danger and I hadn't even meant to.

I rushed toward the driver's side, praying the keys were still in the ignition. I heard a bit of a scuffle and Dee cry out, and I knew that Craig was likely trying to fight his way out of the situation.

If one of them got hurt because of me, I would never forgive myself.

My hand closed over the door handle and I yanked, opening the door. Before I could catapult myself inside, someone grabbed me from behind. His arms were like metal vises, closing around me and locking me in place. I struggled and screamed; I even tried to bite him.

The man brought up a white cloth and stuffed it over my mouth and nose, causing panic to explode through my body like the finale of a Fourth of July firework show.

I couldn't breathe. I was choking. I was going to die.

Automatically, my body searched for oxygen and I sucked in a lungful of air. It was extremely sweet and I noticed the cloth being forced against my face was damp with a dense liquid.

Chloroform.

I began to fight and struggle again, but my movements became sluggish and slow. I felt consciousness loosen as my thoughts began to scatter. I was losing control of my body… I was losing control of this situation.

I blinked, trying to stay awake, trying to focus.

My eyes zeroed in on the keys hanging from the ignition of the Hummer. I had been close. So close.

I went limp in my kidnapper's arms and darkness closed around me.

I hadn't been close enough.

28

Blue

I shook off the men still flanking my sides and took a menacing step toward Dom. "Where is she?" I demanded.

"You're in no position to be making demands."

My fist ached with the need to plow it into his smug face. I no longer cared about bringing this bastard to justice. The only justice for someone like him was the kind he would receive in hell.

"If you hurt her, I will kill you." I vowed.

"Let me tell you how this is going to go," Dom replied, like my promise wasn't something he should even worry about.

I glanced behind him at Slater, wondering when he was going to do something to help.

"He can't help you. No one here can. You just have to do what you're told," Dom said, noting where my gaze had gone.

"What do you want?" I spat.

"I want my drugs. All of them. The entire shipment. Once I have what is mine, I will release the girl."

I snorted. "Like hell. I'm not giving you shit until I see she isn't hurt. I'll give you the drugs when you give me my girl."

Dom stared at me for long moments. "Take me to the drugs and then I'll take you to your girl."

"You think I'm stupid?" I spat. "The minute you see those drugs, you'll kill me and then have her killed. Like I said, you're not even going to lay eyes on that shit 'til I lay eyes on her."

"Fine. We'll trade. You have thirty minutes. Get my stuff and bring it back here."

"Is she here?" I asked, looking past him at the door leading into the house.

"No. But she will be."

I was inclined to believe him because there was no way Slater would just be standing there if Julie was in that house.

"Thirty minutes." I agreed and started walking to my car.

"Slater," Dom ordered behind me. "Go with him. If he tries anything, anything at all, kill him."

"You got it," Slater replied as he followed me down the driveway.

I slammed into the Mustang and revved the engine. The sound of squealing tires and the scent of burning rubber filled the air as I sped away.

As soon as Dom's house was out of sight, I slammed my fist into the dashboard. "What the fuck!"

"You took his shipment?" Slater asked.

"You fucking cold-cocked me in the face." I looked at him.

"If I didn't, it would have looked suspicious."

"Whose side are you on?" I demanded, in no mood for shit.

"The good side."

I wasn't even sure what the good side was anymore. From where I sat, every angle of this case was a freaking clusterfuck.

"Did you know they were going to take Julie?"

"No. What the hell happened?"

"She found his shit," I spat.

"And she's connected to you." Slater whistled through his teeth.

"If he hurts her…" My words trailed away because I couldn't bring myself to finish the sentence.

"I'm sure she's fine. For now," Slater said, subdued.

I felt sick. Physically sick inside. I found the phone I used to call the department and punched the button for Watson. He answered on the first ring.

"We have a hostage situation. I have the drugs in my possession. Dom agreed to make a trade for the goods. We're meeting in less than thirty minutes at his house. I need a team of men ready for a raid."

"Who's the hostage?" Watson said and then started barking orders to the people around him.

"It's Julie," I growled.

Watson paused. "Listen to me, Markson. Don't do anything stupid."

I barked a laugh. I was going to do what I damn well pleased.

"I suggest you get your team ready. Dom and some of the crew will be there, in possession of all their supply. He threatened to kill me. He admitted to killing another member of his crew. I have the location of the body. He kidnapped Julie. We have enough to put him away for life."

If he makes it that long, I added silently.

"We're moving now," Watson said.

Before I could hang up, he called my name.

I didn't say anything.

"Good work, Markson. Let's get this case closed."

I disconnected the call. There was nothing good about any of this.

The old Ford came into view. It was exactly where I left it. I pulled right up beside it and turned to Slater. "Can I trust you?"

His reply was to reach behind him and pull out a Glock, which he extended to me.

"You got one too?"

He lifted his shirt and showed me another identical gun sticking out of the waistband of his jeans. I took the gun he gave me and stuffed it in the waistband of my jeans.

The keys to the truck were right where I left them, and I fired up the engine and sped toward Dom's house. I had just under fifteen minutes to get there, and I hoped this old truck could take the speed I was going to push it.

Slater followed close behind me the entire way. When I turned onto the street of Dom's house, I noticed a new vehicle—black Dodge pickup truck parked in the center of the driveway. My pulse began to hammer and my eyelid began to twitch. I searched the lawn for signs of Julie, and when I didn't see her, I looked at the truck, hoping to see some kind of movement within.

But everything outside was still.

That meant Julie was in that house. In there with a bunch of drug dealers and murderers. I parked the old Ford so close to the black truck that it rocked on its tires when my front fender bumped into it.

As Slater pulled in behind me, I walked toward the garage, which I noticed no longer had a car parked inside.

"Dom!" I yelled, not bothering to be quiet.

The door to the house opened and Dome came out, a few of his crew scattering out behind him like a bunch of ants. "You're late," he said.

"Where is she?" I asked, not bothering to take his bait. I was on time and he damn well knew it.

"Where's the shipment?"

"Outside."

"Pull it into the garage."

"Not until I see Julie."

Slater walked into the garage and stood off to the side, watching.

"Bring her out!" Dom called.

The door to the house opened and two men escorted Julie out. Her wrists were bound together and she had tape over her mouth. Her eyes widened when she saw me, and I couldn't help but note the panicked fear I saw in them.

I tried to keep a lid on my anger. I tried not to let her see how angry and how upset I was that she was dragged into this. All I wanted her to see was my calm exterior so she would know she was safe.

I took a step toward her and two of Dom's guys stepped in my path.

"Move," I growled.

"We have a deal," Dom said.

I tossed the keys at him. They landed at his feet. "Here, get it yourself."

Dom glanced at the man to his right. "Go make sure it's there. Pull it in."

The guy scooped up the keys and went off to do Dom's bidding. I took another step toward Julie. One of the men in my path threw out his fist and connected with my jaw.

Julie's muffled cry snapped something inside me.

I went on autopilot and started fighting. I punched and kicked the two men that dared to block my path. When one tried to hold me, I kicked out and sent the other to his feet.

The sound of a gun cocking is what brought all our heads around. Dom had his gun trained on Julie.

Tentacles of terror wrapped around my body and squeezed. I looked between Julie and the gun, measuring the distance, trying to calculate if I could beat a bullet.

"You'd never make it," Dom said.

The old Ford backed into the garage and everyone looked. Everyone but me and Dom. I kept my eyes on him, while he kept his eyes and gun on Julie.

"Check it," he yelled at Slater.

Slater climbed in the back of the truck and started going through the boxes. "It's here," he called, holding up a bag of cocaine.

I wondered where in the hell my backup was. They should be here by now.

Dom looked at me and I knew he was going to kill us. I didn't have time to wait for the cops to get here. I had to do this on my own.

I pulled out the gun Slater gave me and cocked it, steadily pointing it at Dom. "You so much as sneeze and I will blow your brains out." I vowed.

Every man in the place pulled out a gun, which they trained on me.

I could feel Julie's terror, but I didn't look at her. I kept my eyes on Dom. "You're under arrest for kidnapping, possession, and murder," I said.

Dom's eyes widened.

"He's a narc!" one of the guys yelled, and all hell broke loose.

29

Julie

I don't know how long I was unconscious, but when I woke, my muscles were stiff from being in a heap on the floorboard of the truck they shoved me in.

I also had a thick layer of duct tape binding my wrists and over my mouth. I fought against the panic that squeezed my lungs, reminding myself that I could breathe; I just had to do it through my nose.

I tested and my skin tugged and screamed under the constrictive tape wound tightly around me.

Framed, arrested, and kidnapped all in one day. It had to be some kind of world record.

I lifted my head to take in my surroundings, and I was met with an icy stare. "Don't even try anything," the man said, holding up a gun that was lying in his lap.

I couldn't even ask them where we were going or what was happening because my mouth was sealed closed.

I rested my forehead against the carpet and concentrated on breathing and kept my ears open so I could listen to everything the men said and hopefully learn some answers.

I also thought about Blue. I prayed that he was all right, that he wasn't somehow being hurt too. As much as I hoped he knew what happened to me, I also hoped he didn't. I was afraid of what might happen to him if he tried to save me.

A phone up front rang and someone answered. He barely said two words and then disconnected the call. "We're to meet him," someone said to the driver.

My hip dug into something lying beneath me on the floor as the driver cut a U-turn, the tires squealing on the road. The idiots in the car laughed like they were taking a joy ride on Space Mountain.

A few minutes later, we were pulling up somewhere and stopping.

I was carried into a house, one that stunk like weed and beer, and shoved in an empty closet. It actually was a relief to be left alone, even if it were inside a closet. At least in here I wasn't in a room full of men who were leering at me.

I busied myself trying to loosen the tape that surrounded my wrists, stretching and trying to come up with ways to get it off.

Duct tape was no joke. After fighting with it for a while, I was sweating and my wrists felt raw. I understood why they chose to use this rather than rope. It was better and you could buy it anywhere.

I stiffened when the closet door flung open and I squinted against the sudden bright light. Two men led me through the house and out into the garage.

My eyes went directly to Blue, and relief crashed through me so heavily that I would have moaned if I could. But then I noticed his appearance. He was bloody and bruised. Parts of his face were swollen and one of his hands was scraped up and raw.

What happened to him?

New anxiety pummeled me.

Were we going to get out of this?

Yes, Blue was trained for these kinds of things, but we were sorely outnumbered.

I listened as they flung words back and forth, trying to make sense of it all. They were making a trade. Me for the drugs.

Blue was going to hand over all those drugs just to get me back? Maybe it would have been noble to say—to think—that I wasn't worth all the damage that those drugs could do. Maybe I should have found a way to let Blue know that under no circumstances was he to compromise this case just to save my life.

But I kind of wanted to be saved.

I didn't want to die.

Not here. Not now. Not like this.

The fact that Dom was now holding me at gunpoint only made those feelings stronger.

"You so much as sneeze and I will blow your brains out." Blue growled, pulling out a gun and pointing it at Dom.

Suddenly everyone was holding a gun. Most of them were trained on Blue. I realized then that maybe I was more noble than I thought. Because I was willing to die right now.

If it meant saving Blue.

Knowing that I could die at any moment was probably the scariest feeling I'd ever felt, but fearing that Blue could die?

That was worse.

"You're under arrest for kidnapping, possession, and murder," Blue told Dom, giving away the fact he was undercover.

"He's a narc!" someone yelled as a team of police converged on the house.

Everyone began scrambling around, scattering like leaves in a windstorm. "Cops!" a few yelled as they ran off into the night or back through the house.

The man in the back of the truck jumped down and pulled out a gun that looked just like Blue's. He aimed it right at Dom, who surprisingly hadn't moved.

"Pigs," he spat, looking at Blue and the other man.

"Drop your weapon," Blue ordered as men in black SWAT jackets converged.

I felt the change in the air; I saw the decision in Dom's body before he even acted. Dom swung the gun away from me and aimed it directly at Blue.

And then he pulled the trigger.

I screamed, the sound vibrating my tongue and throat because the tape confined it inside, as I rushed forward, desperate to stop the bullet.

I barely heard the gunfire that erupted around us; I was so intent on getting to Blue.

I wasn't going to make it. I was too far away. I was going to watch a bullet totally destroy my entire life.

The man beside Blue acted fast, jumping in front of Blue and shoving him out of the way. Both men fell, with Blue landing at the bottom.

I made a sound and dropped to my knees beside the men, reaching out with my bound hands, trying to help them, trying to see who was hurt.

A pool of red was rapidly forming around them both, and I desperately wanted to know who was hurt.

Beneath the man Blue shifted and rolled.

"Slater!" Blue said, laying out the man on the ground and bending over him. Slater's shirt was rapidly turning red.

"I need a medic!" Blue roared and then looked back down at the man who literally took a bullet for him.

"You trust me now?" Slater said.

Blue cursed. "You shouldn't have done that."

"Least I could do after you came in here and kicked this case's ass."

Blue made a strangled sound. "Don't you dare die."

"Flesh wound," Slater said as a pair of medics rushed over and began administering first aid.

Blue moved out of their way and turned to me.

Our eyes connected.

His filled with tenderness and mine filled with tears. He pulled me up to my feet and frowned at the tape covering my mouth. Then he ripped it off in one great tear.

"Ow!" I yelled as my skin stung. If I had a mustache, I wouldn't have to worry about bleaching it out ever again.

Blue palmed my face. His skin felt warm against my icy cheeks. He didn't say anything, but he pressed light kisses to the corners of my mouth where the tape had ripped the most. "I'm so sorry," he murmured between kisses.

I brought my still-taped hands between us and gripped his shirt. "Are you okay?"

He looked awful. He was a bloody, swollen mess.

Gently, he folded me into his arms and I pressed my cheek against his chest and sighed. "Yeah, sweetness, I'm just fine now."

Close by, Dom started yelling. "Help me!" he cried. "Can't you see I've been shot!"

Blue pulled back and pinned Dom with a stare. Dom glanced at him and shut up. A paramedic took a few steps toward Dom and Blue shook his head.

"He's low priority. Let him bleed."

Dom started screaming again about police brutality, and Blue turned back to me.

"Guess what?" he said, wrapping me up in his arms once again.

"What?"

"Case is over."

"Hmmm, does that mean you won't stand me up anymore?"

He chuckled. "Are you going to agree to go out with me again?"

"Definitely," I said, dipping my face into his chest. I couldn't keep the smile off my face.

He tipped my chin back with his bruised and bloodied knuckles. "There's just one thing."

I narrowed my eyes. "What?"

"That you're mine. Exclusively."

Joy and warmth filled me up inside. It totally washed away all the bad things that happened and even made me forget I was still bound by duct tape. "I wouldn't have it any other way," I murmured, stretching up on tiptoes so I could kiss him.

It was there in the middle of a drug bust that my happily ever after began.

EPILOGUE

One year later…

The alarm beside my bed went off and I hit the snooze button.

Three times.

When I finally became barely conscious and squinted at the clock, I swore and stumbled out of bed. I was late. Before rushing off into my bathroom I gave a huff at the empty side of the bed—Blue's side. He wasn't there.

So much for blaming him for my tardiness.

Muttering under my breath, I went into the bathroom to wash my face, apply a million types of lotion, and get ready for my day. I would never understand how Blue got up so early in the morning. It was downright wrong.

Yeah, he had to be at work, but even after all this time of living together, I'd never seen him rush around in haste to get there on time. I did it more and more. It was his fault (guess he didn't need to be here to catch the blame after all).

He kept me up way past my bedtime doing things to my body that made it impossible to sleep.

I grinned as I rushed into my closet. Okay, so maybe I didn't mind him keeping me up late. I quickly pulled on a pair of navy-blue linen sailor pants, a fitted red top, and added a long necklace with various glittery golden beads on it.

I rushed back out into the bathroom and reached for my mineral foundation and a brush. Red writing on the mirror stopped me in my tracks.

How had I missed that earlier?

Scrawled across the mirror in my very new, very pricey red lipstick was a note.

Good morning, sleepyhead.

Blue made it absolutely impossible to be mad at him.

I grinned the whole time I applied a basic routine of makeup, then snatched up my supplies to finish my face at work, and rushed down the stairs. No coffee for me this morning; there just wasn't enough time.

Of course, I hit every red light on my way to work. It was annoying, but it gave me time to run a brush through my short, wild mane of hair. It looked more mussed than usual, but I could tame it at work.

When the final light turned green, I breathed a sigh of relief and sped around the turn, pulling onto the street of the salon.

The salon that I owned.

It had always been a dream of mine to open my own shop. To be my own boss. I never thought I could make it happen so soon, but after the Razor's Edge was shut down and Susan lost her cosmetology license, I decided I didn't want to try to find a job at someone else's salon.

Susan was lucky, though, because she avoided jail time. Her testimony along with all the evidence Blue and Slater collected put Dom and his crew away for a very long time. And of course, Dom wasn't going to go down alone, and he took LeBraun and some of the Myrtle Beach crew down with him. The streets were cleaner and kids were safer thanks to Blue and the hard work of the JPD.

After a couple weeks of time off for both of us (mostly spent in bed), Blue went back to work on the force, and I opened up my own business. Right now there was only me and two other girls working there, but I planned to hire more. Our calendars were filling up quickly.

Pretty soon, *Shear Perfection Salon* was going to be the hottest place in town to get your hair styled.

The flashing of red-and-blue lights in my rearview mirror caught my attention and I groaned. Up the street, the sign for my shop beckoned, and I momentarily entertained the idea of ignoring the cop and just going ahead to work.

I had a feeling Blue wouldn't approve.

As I pulled to the side of the street, I wondered if being the girlfriend of a cop would get me a warning instead of a ticket.

Once the car was in park, I turned, digging around in my bag for my license. A knock on the window had me turning around.

I knew that torso anywhere.

I slid down the window. "Is there a problem, officer?" I asked innocently.

"I have it on good authority that you were warned once before about speeding through an intersection, ma'am."

I bit back a grin. "Normally I don't speed. But I have this boyfriend who likes to keep me up half the night, and I overslept… I'm late for work."

"You should get rid of that guy. He sounds like trouble."

"Maybe I like trouble."

Blue chuckled and leaned down and rested his elbows on the ledge of the open window. "Hi."

Even after a year, he still made my insides tremble. "Hey."

And damn could he fill out a uniform.

He pinned me with a stern look. "You were speeding, Jules."

I sighed heavily. "You gonna give me a ticket?"

"I'm prepared to let you off with a warning." He grinned. "On one condition."

I raised an eyebrow. "Well, by all means, tell me what I need to do, *officer.*"

Before I could even blink, a black velvet box appeared between us. I gasped and looked up into his face. He leaned a little farther into the window.

"I've been carrying this around for a while now…" He began and cleared his throat. I stared at the little square box as my hands began to tremble.

I didn't want to get ahead of myself, but I couldn't help but notice that it was the perfect size for a diamond ring.

I held my breath as he slowly lifted the lid.

The early morning sunlight reflected off the diamond, instantly setting it into a glittering fire. I gasped as my hand pressed against my chest.

It was simply stunning.

A large round diamond—at least a carat in weight—surrounded by much smaller diamonds circling the large center stone. It was set in platinum and the band was ultra thin and light.

"Blue?" I whispered, tearing my eyes away from the ring and to look into his face.

"Marry me, Julie."

My heart was beating so hard against my chest that I couldn't draw a breath. I just sat there staring… *feeling*.

He was offering me the thing I wanted most in this life.

Him. Forever.

I must have sat there too long because he cleared his throat. "Julie?"

My eyes snapped up to his. How many times had I gotten lost in those blue depths? "Yeah?"

"Would you rather have a ticket than this ring?"

"No!" I cried. Was he insane?

"So you gonna give me an answer?" He half smiled.

"Yes!"

"Yes, you're going to give me an answer or…?" His words fell away. I opened my door in a burst of thrilled energy.

Blue groaned and bent when the door hit him.

"Oh!" I cried, slipping out of the car. "Blue!" I grabbed his arm to see if he was okay.

"Speeding *and* assaulting an officer," he said, straightening and looking down into my face. "I'm gonna have to take you in, ma'am."

"Yes," I said. There wasn't a hint of doubt anywhere in my voice. I was absolutely sure. Marrying Blue was going to be a dream come true.

"Yes?" Blue said, stepping closer to me.

"A million times, yes."

He grinned and swept me up into his arms against his solid frame. "I don't think I've ever been so nervous," he murmured into my hair.

I pulled back to look up at him. "You thought I would say no?"

"Well, you can be pretty grouchy in the morning," he quipped.

I smacked his chest and laughed. "Give me that ring."

"With pleasure," he said, removing its glittery beauty from the black velvet and taking my left hand.

Cars whizzed by on the street beside us, but I didn't hear them. The only thing I saw and heard was Blue.

"I love you, Julie," he said, sliding the cool platinum band over my knuckle, placing it exactly where it belonged.

I didn't even look at the stone. My free hand curved up around his neck and drew his face down so I could kiss him. His lips were giving and moist, soft and generous. The way we moved together was like we were perfectly in sync. The buttons on his shirt pressed into my chest as I crushed myself closer and the hat on his head fell by our feet when my hands slid up to tangle in his hair.

Behind us, cars began to honk. He broke the kiss, laughing at the chaos we were causing.

"Someone's going to crash," he said.

I smiled and pulled my hand up between us, taking in the engagement ring on my finger. It was absolutely gorgeous. It was the most beautiful piece of jewelry I'd ever seen. "Did you pick this? It's perfect."

"You're happy?" he asked, snaking a hand around my hip.

"Oh, yes," I said, tipping my chin upward. "I'm so happy."

He tugged on a piece of wayward hair. "Good."

"What about you?" I asked. "You happy?"

"I could be better…" he said with a smile.

"Oh yeah? Tell me, future husband, how could you be better?" I asked as heat coiled in my belly. I was going to be *really* late for work today.

"Kiss me," he murmured, already placing his lips upon mine.

It was the kiss that marked the beginning of the rest of our life.

The End

You lucky dog, you. Not only did you just get to read **TIPSY** but now you get a sneak peek of **Tricks**, written by Cambria Hebert!
Turn the page for the fun to begin!

TRICKS

(a *Take It Off* novel)

Love can play tricks on your heart…

After serving several years in the United States Marine Corps, Sergeant Tucker Patton decides to hang up his uniform and go to work at a private investigative firm owned by his buddy. His boxes are packed and he's got one foot out the door when a phone call changes everything.

Instead of going to North Carolina, he heads to New York City to literally step into the life of his twin brother, who died under suspicious circumstances. But pretending to be someone else isn't easy.

Especially when the person you're supposed to be is wanted dead.

Not only that, but he's going from being blissfully single to living with his brother's woman. An uptight, no-nonsense lawyer.

Charlotte Rose Carter doesn't have time for fun and games. She graduated with honors and made all the right moves fresh out of college to jumpstart her career as a successful young lawyer. She even snagged the most eligible bachelor in New York City's corporate world.

So what if her and Max's relationship isn't burning up the sheets? So what if their life doesn't read like a chapter from a sizzling romance novel? This is the real world, and in the real world that stuff is just fantasy.

Until it isn't.

Suddenly, just the slightest touch or a single glance from Max has her heart doing somersaults. Suddenly, the lackluster relationship begins to spark, and Charlotte finds herself tied in a knot of desire.

But she has no idea about the tricks being played right under her perky little nose.

Turn the page for Chapter One of *Tricks*.

TRICKS

Sneak Peek

1

Tucker

My mouth felt like it was packed with cotton. You know that dry but slightly sticky feeling? My tongue moved and it brushed against the roof of my mouth, and the cotton came with it.

I grunted and opened my eyes, only to immediately shut them again. I wasn't ready for morning. *Shit, how much did I drink last night?* My body was still heavy with sleep, my limbs not wanting to cooperate.

One of my arms was flung wide and I pulled it in to rub a hand over my sleepy face, hoping it would wake me up a little more. I knew I needed to get up… I just couldn't think of the reason.

Something shifted beside me and I felt the covers lift and drop. The soft sound of footsteps reached my ears. It wasn't a something. It was a *someone.*

I went home with someone last night.

Opening my eyes again, I glanced to my left in time to see a woman wearing nothing but a pink thong step into the adjoining bathroom and quietly close the door. Well, now I remembered the reason I went home with her.

Her ass was luscious.

Vague memories of last night filtered through my hazy, beer-soaked memory of skin against skin and a low seductive laugh. What was her name again? Veronica? Violet? Shit, I hadn't a clue.

Tossing away the covers, I swung my legs over the side of the mattress and looked down. I was buck-ass naked. I looked around for my clothes, which were lying in a pile near the door of the bedroom.

Must have been in a hurry to get naked. I smirked. I was always in a hurry to get naked. Especially when I was with a woman with an ass like that.

I glanced back at the closed bathroom door as the toilet flushed and the tap water turned on. That was my cue to leave. I had on my boxers and jeans before the door opened.

Rushing out the door with shirt in hand seemed a little immature, so I turned. And, man, did I get an eyeful. There was no way in hell her boobs were real. They were too perfect. Large round, creamy globes sat high atop her chest. They gave way to a flat stomach with a light-reflecting stud in her bellybutton. The pink thong was still in place but left little to imagination, and her long, tan legs stretched all the way to the floor.

Her hair was dark, her features exotic, and her lips were full.

Even drunk, I had great taste.

I motioned with my chin, a little *what's up* gesture, and draped my T-shirt over my shoulder.

"Leaving so soon?" she asked, padding across the carpeting toward me.

I didn't even pretend to not look at her chest. Shit, this had been a one-night stand. She could think I was a dog all she wanted. Hell, she'd be right.

'Course, she clearly wasn't the type of girl to be offended by my wandering eyes. She walked right up to me, wound her arms around my bare waist, and pressed those perfect tits right up against my chest. Then she rubbed around like she was a cat and I was her scratching pole.

"Don't you want to stay for breakfast?" she purred.

"Much as I'd like to, I can't. Got somewhere to be."

The woman whose name might or might not be Veronica pulled back and sashayed her ass across the room to a wooden nightstand by the bed. She bent at the waist, giving me the perfect view of said bottom as she scrawled something on a piece of paper.

I considered staying longer, but if I did that, she'd think this wasn't just a one-night stand. Girls were complicated like that. If our night stretched into morning, they got ideas. Ideas that maybe they would be the one to capture the guy no one else could. They would read something more into morning sex than the sex that occurred late at night when both our tongues tasted of beer.

I might sleep around, I might like a variety of ladies, but I never gave false hope where there was none. I might be a dog, but I wasn't an ass.

Sweet cheeks (I had to call her something) swayed her hips back across the room and held out a scrap of paper to me. "Call me," she said, flipping her hair behind her shoulder.

I glanced at her chest one more time, then stuffed the piece of paper in the front pocket of my jeans.

She leaned up and pressed her lips to mine, slipping her tongue between. I kissed her back quickly and then slowly pulled away. Reaching around, I palmed her ass. "Thanks for last night," I said and walked out of her bedroom without even looking back.

By the front door, I found my shoes and leather jacket and quickly finished dressing before stepping out into the cold morning air. I wasn't going to miss this cold. I was actually looking forward to moving on, trying something new.

A thin layer of frost covered the windshield on my truck. Instead of getting out and scraping it, I blasted the heat and let the engine idle, letting it melt on its own. While I waited, I pulled out the already crumpled piece of paper I was just given. Smoothing it out, I looked down, my eyes skimming over the number I was never going to call to look for her name.

I laughed and crumpled the paper back up and tossed in on the floor of the truck.

Rachel.

Damn. I hadn't even been close.

Ready for more? Tucker and Charlotte's story will be available in early 2014!

ACKNOWLEDGEMENTS

(Note from the Author)

Dear Diary,

I went to the store today and wandered around for hours and ended up buying three bottles of nail polish and some nail art decals so I could do my nails like all those pictures I have seen on Pinterest.

Oh wait. This isn't my diary.

But you know that little tidbit above describes perfectly my attention span while I was writing this book. Yes, I know. I just practically called myself out in my own book. But hey, I'm nothing if I'm not honest. And I think we established several books ago that my "acknowledgements" were going to be more of a note from me about what I was up to and experiencing while I wrote each book.

So what does this have to do with nail polish?

Just the fact that this poor book has experienced just about every single type of writer ADD that a book could possibly suffer. I actually got the idea for this book YEARS ago. I've been sitting on it because it never felt like a right time to sit down and write it. I had this idea before I wrote *Heven & Hell*. In fact, I would go out on a limb to say that this was one of my first book ideas. Now, I have a lot of ideas. A lot of them, sadly, come and go. But the best ideas, the characters who beg to be given a book, stick around. This book did just that. It sat and waited for its turn until I realized it would fit perfectly with the *Take It Off* series.

So Julie and Blue were born. I just love the name Blue.

Anyway, I intended to release this book before *Text*. It was originally due to be the fourth *Take It Off* novel. Halfway through writing this book, Honor and Nathan literally took over my mind. At first I fought it. I remember whenever I was running or driving or cooking or doing whatever I did, I was constantly thinking up new book ideas. Characters were springing themselves on me left and right. It was frankly maddening. I'm the kind of writer who likes to write one book at a time. I don't like to have multiple projects going. I like to give my characters their own attention, their own unique voice. For me, I feel like if I'm writing two or three books at once, then the voices are going to overlap whether I want them to or not.

So I fought all those storyline ideas. I fought the voices. I wrote them down… I ignored them.

They won anyway.

Honor would not be pushed aside. So… I opened up a new doc and started *Text*. I wrote until it was done. Julie and Blue were on hold.

So after I finished *Text* I came back to *Tipsy*. Interesting factoid here… I was so indecisive on the title of this book. It was originally going to be called *Tangled* ('cause you know she's a stylist and hair gets tangled and she gets tangled in crime). But there are a lot of books out with that title already. So then I changed it to *Tame*, because one day I was washing my hair in the shower and thought to myself, *Shampoo your crazy hair good and tame that crap!* Then I was all like, ooh! That's what I'll call it.

Seriously.

I shouldn't title books while washing my hair in the shower.

I had *Tipsy* on my list of possible titles for the series and I knew I was going to use it, but I had planned on using it for another book. But then Julie started saying that word. As in, "You can't get tipsy off a person."

And that's how this book got its title. Julie picked it.

Anyway, back to my interesting story. I know you are totally into this.

So after I changed the title three times, stopped halfway to write *Text* and then came back to *Tipsy*… I started writing. And then another set of characters totally started pestering me.

They pestered me enough that I wrote the prologue and the first chapter.

Yep.

I am officially insane.

Then I closed that document and told myself I. Would. Finish. TIPSY.

This is where the nail polish comes in. And the baking. And the cleaning. And the social media stalking.

Yep. I pretty much did everything but write.

Except clean my bathrooms. I'm still putting that off. Ha ha ha ha.

The days rolled by and then one day, I looked at the calendar and realized time was no longer on my side. I had deadlines. It was time to get real.

And so I finished. I hope you like the end result. ☺

After all that, I figure I probably need a mini break… Oh look, something shiny….

wanders away......
See you next book!

Cambria Hebert is the author of the young adult paranormal *Heven and Hell* series, the new adult *Death Escorts* series, and the new adult *Take it Off* series. She loves a caramel latte, hates math, and is afraid of chickens (yes, chickens). She went to college for a bachelor's degree, couldn't pick a major, and ended up with a degree in cosmetology. So rest assured her characters will always have good hair. She currently lives in North Carolina with her husband and children (both human and furry), where she is plotting her next book. You can find out more about Cambria and her work by visiting http://www.cambriahebert.com.

"Like" her on Facebook:
https://www.facebook.com/pages/Cambria-Hebert/128278117253138
Follow her on Twitter: https://twitter.com/cambriahebert
Pinterest: https://pinterest.com/cambriahebert/pins/
GoodReads:
http://www.goodreads.com/author/show/5298677.Cambria_Hebert
Cambria's website: http://www.cambriahebert.com

Cambria Hebert